It is 1192 and the orphaned Lady Judith of Claverham has joined the Third Crusade in a desperate search for her only brother Edwin. What hope has a lone woman against the Saracen hordes? Soon after landing in the Holy Land she is captured by a band of marauding soldiers and only the intervention of King Richard's handsome knight, Geoffrey de Belgarde, saves her from the harem of the Saracen Prince Hasan.

Then through her own folly she endangers the life of Sir Geoffrey and, to save him from certain death at the hands of the Turks, Lady Judith is forced to become his wife—she who has sworn she would rather marry a serpent than anyone bearing the name of de Belgarde.

Lady of the Moon

Alex Andrews

MILLS & BOON LIMITED
London · Sydney · Toronto

First published in Great Britain 1983
by Mills & Boon Limited, 15–16 Brook's Mews,
London W1A 1DR

ISBN 0 263 74242 3

Set in 10 on 12 pt Linotron Times
04/0483

Photoset by Rowland Phototypesetting Ltd
Bury St Edmunds, Suffolk
Made and printed in Great Britain by
Cox & Wyman Ltd, Reading

Mediterranean Sea

ACRE ✠

Sea of Galilee

Nazareth

marshy plain

MEGIDDO ◉

EMPIRE OF SALADIN

OUTREMER

JAFFA ✠

Ascalon ✠

Jerusalem ◉

Dead Sea

✠ Darum

0   10   20 miles

⊕ Captured or already held by Crusaders

◉ Saracen-held

The boundary between Outremer (the Crusaders' 'Land Beyond the Sea') and Saladin's Empire is meant only as a rough guide.

CHAPTER
ONE

JUDITH of Claverham sat at her tapestry frame, plying the needle without thought for the task. Through a window September sunlight shafted across the rushes on the floor and the breeze brought the sound of the younger nuns and novices enjoying their hour of relaxation, but inside the Priory all was still, thick walls keeping the air cool.

A patter of sandalled feet brought Judith out of bitter thoughts as the Almoner, Sister Maud, appeared in the doorway, her plump body clad in the black habit of her order and her face flushed against the white wimple beneath her hood.

'Lady Judith,' she panted. 'The Prioress asks you to present yourself at the outer parlour. There's a visitor asking for you.'

Surprise made Judith careless. The needle bit deep and, wincing, she sucked at the spot of blood that welled on her forefinger. 'A visitor for me? Who, Sister?'

'Earl Torquil of Brecon!' came the awed whisper.

Judith caught her breath, her blue eyes narrowing. 'What does he want?'

'He says his message is for your ears alone, my lady. Will you come quickly, please? You know how the Prioress feels about male visitors.'

Sister Maud scurried away, her feet scuffing in the passage, and Judith stood up, hands clenched around folds of her skirt. She was a slender girl lately turned eighteen, wearing a loose blue gown which draped softly over her curves except where it was caught in a leather girdle encircling her waist. Hair of a pale silver-gold hung in two thick braids from beneath a veil held on her brow by a bronze circlet, and though her face was white with apprehension her eyes had darkened to a stormy violet.

Almost a year had passed since her father's untimely death, after which her young brother Edwin, heir to Claverham, had been taken into Earl Torquil's household to serve as a squire until he came of age. Meanwhile his inheritance had come into the hands of Earl Torquil, who as their overlord had total power over Judith and her brother. Judith, without a dowry, had been sent to moulder as a guest at the Priory of St Agnes. How dared Earl Torquil now intrude on her retreat? Judith and think of no reason for this visit—unless some ill had befallen her brother.

Suddenly fearing for Edwin's safety, she hurried down the passage and approached the door of the outer parlour, pausing a moment to adjust her veil and square her shoulders before lifting the latch. Her visitor stared out of the window, one foot on a painted chest and his cloak caught up on the sword which tilted from his left hip. He was apparently watching the activity in the courtyard, where a peasant struggled to turn an ox-cart, and the sight must have amused him for as he turned he was smiling cynically. Judith felt as though pure evil had stepped into the heart of the Priory, for she hated this thin, grey-haired man with all her heart. A lifetime of cruelty had driven deep lines into his face, and it was the face of an eagle, cold and predatory.

'My lady.' The Earl made her a formal bow, his cloak sweeping to the rush-strewn floor, his jewels glinting in the sunlight. 'How are you faring?'

In reply, Judith dipped the merest suggestion of a curtsey. 'Well enough, my lord. What news of my brother?'

'Ah, yes. Young Edwin.' He studied a garnet ring that glowed like blood on his finger. 'I fear you may be distressed to learn that he has run away from Castle Belgarde, along with his serf Magnus.'

'Run away?' Judith breathed. 'But why?'

'It seems he has been talking of following the King to the Holy Land,' he replied, heavy-lidded eyes fixed on her face, which turned white as bleached linen.

'He's gone on Crusade?' she got out. 'But he's only fifteen!'

'Younger men than he have gone,' Earl Torquil said. 'Your brother is not the only one who wishes to be present when King Richard enters the Holy City.'

Laying a hand to her spinning head, Judith sank down on one of the chests that furnished the room. 'But haven't you sent after him, my lord? Could you do nothing to stop him?'

'By now he could be aboard ship at any one of a dozen ports,' the Earl said with a shrug.

She guessed he was not displeased by this development. Edwin's departure rid him of the troublesome presence of another member of the Claverham family, whose rich lands he had long coveted. Despairingly she thought of her brother, who was as fair as she but small for his age; a delicate lad gone like a sacrificial offering to the Saracen sword, somewhere in a far foreign land called Outremer, the land beyond the sea.

'When a man hears the call of the Cross it is his duty to go,' the Earl said, thus relieving himself of all responsibility in the matter. 'As for yourself, my dear Judith . . . The Prioress tells me you have no vocation, nor the humility to accept a life of devotion to the church. Since that is the case, I believe you will welcome the alternative I offer.'

'Which is?' she asked, still numb with shock.

Extending a hand intended to convey his concern and care, Torquil smiled at her—an expression marred by the cold calculation in his eyes. 'The only other course open to a lady of gentle birth, my dear. Marriage.'

The word brought her to her feet, colour ebbing and flowing in her face while her thoughts beat inside her head like bats around a cave. Since she had no dowry, marriage was out of the question—unless Edwin died, in which case she would inherit the Claverham lands and become a rich prize. *That* was the Earl's evil intent!

'You dare to come here and offer me your hand?' she said hoarsely.

'I?' he exclaimed with a short laugh. 'Indeed, my dear, you flatter me. I am past the age when I should care to marry again. But I do have sons. Sir Waldin is, of course, my heir and will wed a lady of his own station. But Geoffrey . . . I dare say you will do well enough for Geoffrey.'

She was silent, hating him for being so certain that Edwin would perish. She had heard of his younger son

Geoffrey, a mercenary knight without inheritance of his own, who hired his sword to any lord willing to pay. He, too, was tainted with brutality and wickedness, for the Earl's black blood ran in his veins.

Shaking with contained fright and fury, she said in a low voice, 'I would as soon wed with a serpent. Should my brother die, I shall renounce all claim to Claverham. You may take my lands, but I deny you the right to claim my person, too.'

'As you please,' he replied with indifference. 'But do not forget that I gave you the choice.'

As he strode past her to the door she drew her skirts aside, unwilling for them to brush against him. She hated him with all her heart and soul—him and his evil sons. Please God that Edwin returned in safety!

A feeling of helplessness held Judith in thrall. Without a father or a husband, a woman could do little to change her fate. At night she wept beneath the thin blanket that covered her pallet, and her days passed in a haze of misery as she thought of the perils which Edwin must encounter. Her only consolation was the fact that the serf Magnus had gone with him. A giant of a man, red-haired and bearded, Magnus had been Edwin's faithful guard since the lad was a babe.

She thought often of taking the veil, but she had no vocation for a life of prayer. She missed the squabbles and laughter of family and servants around her, a rich life ordered by the seasons. Here at the Priory each day was the same as the last, a routine regulated by bells. However hard she tried, Judith could not resign herself to spending the rest of her life in that way.

Soon after Christmas, news came that King Richard Coeur de Lion was preparing to march on Jerusalem from one of the Crusader bases on the coast of Judea. Everyone talked of the brave deeds of the King and of the courage of the ladies who accompanied him, including his young Queen Berengaria of Navarre and his sister the Lady Joan. And then, amongst the gossip, Judith caught the sentence that seemed to answer all her prayers: because of King Richard's successes in battle, the coastal towns of the Holy Land were open again to ships bearing pilgrims.

Unable to contain herself, Judith went to the Prioress's private apartments and found the old woman huddled beneath a fur rug with a cup of mulled wine in her hands and not far away a bronze warming-bowl contained a piece of smouldering charcoal to warm the air. The shutters were closed against the chill winter fog and candlelight flickered on a gold crucifix against the white wall.

'My old bones feel the cold,' the Prioress said with a smile, indicating a stool. 'Sit down, Judith, my dear child. Have you come to tell me you are ready to take your vows?'

Judith flushed, muttering, 'No, holy mother. I fear my heart is too much with the real world. Forgive me, I—' About to launch into more excuses, she looked across and saw that the Prioress was smiling, her eyes deep-set and twinkling in the shadow of her hood. Judith thought, as she had often thought in the past, that the old nun knew far more about her than she ought to know. 'I have come, holy mother, to tell you that I wish to go on a pilgrimage. To Outremer.'

The Prioress sat quite still, her smile dying. 'To the Holy Land? A pilgrimage of faith?'

'Yes, holy mother.'

Reaching to put down her cup, the old woman turned to face Judith fully, candlelight illuminating her lined face and her intense eyes. 'Have you any idea how dangerous such a journey may be? The sea voyage is arduous. There may be storms. And if you reach the Holy Land you will have only your grey robe of pilgrimage to protect you from the Infidel. These Saracens are fierce and they abhor Christians.'

'Even so, I intend to go,' Judith said. 'Anyone may make a pilgrimage. I do not fear the dangers.'

'But you have no money, child. How will you pay for your passage? Will you be herded with common peasants, crammed like cattle aboard a small vessel with little food and water, where disease may ravage you?'

'I don't care how I go! I only know I must go!'

A draught from somewhere caused the candle flame to duck and weave, sending shadows dancing across the wall, and for a while the Prioress sat immobile, her eyes fixed on Judith's face.

'I, too,' she said eventually, 'would like to see Jerusalem before I die. I am an old woman, and weary, but I feel the call to go to the holy places. If I should die in the attempt, I shall be content.'

Judith held her breath, hardly daring to believe her ears. She saw the Prioress smile gently, sadly.

'Ah, Judith,' came the sigh. 'I know what draws you on this quest. For you the call is an earthly one. It is your brother, is it not? You have been unsettled ever since a certain nobleman came to visit you.'

Judith felt her face burn. The old nun seemed to be reading her mind, and obviously she listened to gossip, too. 'I am afraid for my brother,' she admitted. 'He is so young—and I am all the family he has. I must know what has become of him.'

'I understand,' the Prioress said softly. 'I, too, had a brother once. Very well, we shall go, you and I, and as many of the nuns as have courage to accompany us. Never doubt that your quest will need great courage, as well as faith.'

'I know that, holy mother,' Judith said, but her eyes shone. Now she would find Edwin and bring him home. That was all that really mattered.

On a day in May in the year 1192, Judith stood on the prow of a merchant ship and watched as the Holy Land came into view, hills lying like cloudbanks along the horizon. Around her other pilgrims peered at the sight, pointing and chattering, but Judith stood a little apart, unable to share the uncomplicated joy of the peasants.

It was more than two months since she had left the shores of England in company with the Prioress and three of the nuns of St Agnes. Several pieces of gold had bought them the benefit of a tent stretched across the deck, but the deprivations of the voyage had soon begun to tell on the oldest member of their party. As the weeks passed the Prioress had grown more frail, though her gentle smile never wavered, however hard the wind might blow or the seas heave. Then, as they came to harbour in Cyprus before the final leg of the journey, it had become clear that the old woman could go no further. She had had to be carried ashore and in the shelter of a nunnery she had died peacefully, still smiling. The three younger nuns had lost heart and decided to stay behind on the island, so Judith had continued alone, borne up by her determination to find Edwin though she sorely missed the consolation of the Prioress's company.

As the warm wind billowed the sail, driving the ship rapidly towards the land, the hills behind the coast turned to green and gold. Shading her eyes with her hand, Judith saw the town which was their destination. It stood on a promontory of land, its white buildings shining in the sunlight which glinted on strange domes and towers, with palm trees lending their dark green to the scene. In the harbour, merchant ships and war galleys vied for room with smaller craft swarming round like insects, and from the strong defensive towers there waved the scarlet banners of Richard of England.

'Is this Acre?' the lad beside Judith asked.

'I believe so, Tom,' she replied, grateful for his friendship. She suspected him to be a rascal who regarded the golden town of Acre as a place for rich pickings, though he had never attempted to touch the purse which hung at her girdle, where she kept a small store of money given to her by the Prioress. In a strange way, Tom seemed to feel that he and she were kindred spirits since he, too, was alone.

'Is the King here?' he wanted to know.

'He may be,' Judith said.

As the anchor rattled down into the harbour, several long rowing boats made for the ship and the master called his passengers to gather to be ferried ashore. Judith was carried along in the crush of eager bodies, clutching her bundle of belongings. Several hands helped her over the side and down into the shallow craft below, with Tom coming monkey-fashion after her. A warm wind brought strange scents to her nostrils, oddly exotic after weeks of the stench of dirty, sweating bodies around her. Everything was new and strange. What waited for her here? Would she find Edwin?

Rather than making for the wharfside, the boat headed for a cave-like entrance among some rocks, from where a tunnel stretched back beneath the town. By the entrance a monk waited with a flaming torch, his black habit adorned on the breast with the white cross of St John.

'Welcome,' he called cheerfully, extending a hand to help the passengers alight since most of them were unsteady on their feet. Judith's legs ached as she gained the rocky floor of the tunnel and peered into the darkness, sharing the half-joyful, half-fearful feelings of her companions.

Lit by the flicker of the monk's torch, they scuffed and stumbled their way along the passage, coming at last to a huge vaulted hall built beneath ground, where more kindly monks waited to give each pilgrim a bowl of thick broth and a hunk of bread. Judith was similarly rewarded and, feeling pangs of hunger gnaw at her stomach, she took her place on the floor with the rest and began to eat. Soon, she thought, she would decide what her next step ought to be, but for the moment it was enough to rest where the floor did not rock beneath her, though the crush of other bodies had begun to feel stifling.

The monks, all bearing the white cross on their habits,

came round distributing grey cloaks, which all pilgrims
were advised to wear to identify their purpose in Outremer. Judith stiffly rose to her feet, tossing off her own
dark mantle to change it for the thin grey one. Her gown
was stained and crumpled and she had not washed her
face for days, but at least the grey cloak was clean, if
neatly-darned. She whirled it about her shoulders, tied
the strings at her throat, arranged her veil—and, suddenly aware that she was being watched, looked over the
heads of a group of seated pilgrims and met the bright,
interested eyes of a dark-faced knight.

He was very tall, wearing silver chain-mail beneath a
tunic and cloak which bore the same insignia as the
monks' garments, and the hood-piece of his armour was
thrown back, revealing tousled dark hair around that
face so deeply browned by the Judean sun. Even from
that distance, Judith was startled to see eyes that seemed
to glow like those of a wild-cat, fringed by dark lashes
that looked almost too beautiful in a man. But the rest of
him was all male, sturdy and muscular, and Judith found
herself disturbed by his scrutiny.

Realising that it was her circlet which had drawn his
attention, she pulled the hood of the cloak up around her
head and turned away, seeing that Tom, sitting by her
feet, was hungrily scraping her broth bowl with the last
crust of his bread. When she glanced back at the knight
he had moved away to converse with two of his com-
rades.

She sat down again, as if to hide herself in the crowd,
and saw that Tom was watching the three armoured
soldiers with interest.

'Are they the King's men?' he asked.

'Not exactly,' she replied. 'Those white crosses mark them as Knights of St John. They help to guard the castles and take care of pilgrims like us.'

Her eyes strayed once again to the tall, dark-haired man and a frown creased her brows. These Hospitallers, like the Templars, were all men of God, having taken an oath to observe monastic vows, remain without possessions, and to be celibate. Such men had no right to look at women as this one, with the disturbing eyes and stubborn chin, had looked at her.

She considered his ruffled hair and tanned profile as he spoke earnestly with his companions, and she caught herself thinking that it was a pity such a man should confine himself to the harsh, ascetic life of a soldier-monk.

'I'm off to explore,' Tom said, getting to his feet. 'Are you coming, lady?'

'I would welcome some fresh air,' Judith said. 'It's too hot in here.'

Gathering up her bundle, she forced her aching legs to straighten, shook out her skirts, and could not resist another glance at the knight. He was watching her again, and as their eyes met she flushed scarlet and turned away to follow Tom to the corner where stairs circled up towards sunlight.

The noise of a hundred chattering voices reached her long before she gained the top of the stairs and looked out across a teeming, busy bazaar. Men in many different costumes, their skins shading from white to ebony, moved or stood or leaned, while the women all seemed to be garbed in black which covered everything but their eyes. A few armoured knights rode through the throng, heading a column of men-at-arms, and a small train of laden donkeys came by on its way to the harbour. Judith caught the sound of foreign tongues and breathed deeply of the strong and unfamiliar scents of the East.

Among the wares on display she saw figs and dates, with other things she could not name. In another place a man sold animal skins, alongside spices, rolls of rainbow-hued materials of lightest weave, and beads and bangles . . .

How was she to find Edwin in this strange place? A vast army was garrisoned in the Holy Land, at the coastal towns and in castles further inland—that much she had learned on Cyprus. Jerusalem itself remained in the hands of the Infidel Sultan, Saladin, but the Crusaders were in possession of many other places. Edwin might be anywhere.

'Come, Tom,' she said, and glanced around only to find that Tom had slipped away. Sighing, she decided that the lad was well able to care for himself—more able than she, in all probability. She only hoped he would not be tempted to steal from the wondrous display in the bazaar.

No one took much notice of one more grey-robed pilgrim as Judith set out to explore the town and get her bearings. She walked down twisting lanes between high walls, with here and there a glimpse of a courtyard with vines twining beside a door, or a whiff of foreign cooking. Horsemen came and went, but most of the people were on foot, engaged in their own business.

Twilight caught her unawares, in an area of the town where the buildings still showed damage after the recent siege. The only people in sight appeared to be soldiers, who looked at her sidelong. Lights began to flicker as the daylight waned, and male voices shouted raucously. Not far away, someone was singing an obscene ditty.

As she hesitated, a man appeared at a gateway between crumbling walls, a skin of wine in one hand, his eyes glazed.

'Hey, look here!' he called, and several more lurching figures appeared. The man lunged at Judith, catching her arm as she backed away. 'What have you got in that bundle?'

'My belongings,' she said, pulling against the hand that gripped her arm. 'Let me go, you drunken oaf!'

'Oaf, is it?' He swung her round against the wall, fumbling at her clothing. As she fought to fend him off she dropped her bundle and was dimly aware that his companions had pounced on it. But more important was the assault on her person. Foul breath made her jerk her head away as he bent over her and she felt a whiskered chin brush her cheek. Her hood fell back, and the sight of her youth and comeliness proved a spur to the ruffian's drunken passion. Despite her struggles his lips came on her throat.

'Hold, there!' a new voice roared. 'Hold, I say!'

Released from her attacker's questing paws, Judith leaned weakly against the wall, grateful to hear the rasp of a sword drawn from its sheath behind her. The soldiers scattered among the shadowed buildings and Judith saw what remained of her belongings—a thin white chemise, now torn and trampled into the dust and filth. Instinctively she felt for the purse at her girdle and found it still there, still with its small weight of gold.

'Lady, what are you doing here?' the newcomer demanded. He, at least, had the grace to notice her bronze circlet.

She turned to thank him, but the words died in her throat as she saw the grim face and flashing, lynx-like eyes of the knight she had seen in the crypt. Astonishment held her silent, one hand braced against the wall while the other clasped the grey cloak at her throat.

'God's blood!' the knight swore harshly. 'Have you no thought for your safety? Did you expect to find chivalry in the heart of the garrison quarter?'

Judith stared at him, affronted not so much by what he said as by the fact that he, a soldier-monk dedicated to the church, should use such oaths and speak to a lady in that rough fashion.

'I did not know it was the garrison area,' she protested.

With an impatient movement he lifted his sword and thrust it back into its scabbard, growling, 'Ignorance should have made you more cautious, not less so. Where are your companions?'

'I have none,' she said wearily, wishing herself back at the crypt. Even a thin pallet crammed between other sleeping pilgrims would seem like a mattress of down to her tired bones.

'None?' he repeated incredulously. 'You came alone—all the way from England?'

'No, I—I came with my friends the nuns of St Agnes, but they stayed behind on Cyprus Island when the Prioress died. Oh, sir, I'm very tired. Will you take me back to the crypt of St John?'

'Aye. Come.' As if sensing that she was on the point of collapse, he took her arm and led her away.

Overhead the stars blinked on one by one. Judith and her escort passed shadowy figures in flowing robes and encountered a squad of guards who saluted the knight. His hand remained beneath her arm, though it was hard to tell whether he was supporting her or forcing her along, irritated by the slowness of her pace.

'Let me rest a moment!' she gasped eventually. Shaking free of his grip, she leaned tiredly on the nearest wall, where some climbing plant hung down, its leaves swaying in the cool night breeze. Faint starlight gleamed on her companion's dark hair, but she could not see his face clearly. Stifling tears, she massaged the sole of her foot, where a stone had cut through her thin shoe.

'You should never have come to Outremer,' the knight said impatiently. 'This is no place for a lady alone.'

'I had to come. I must find my brother.'

As if drawn by the distress in her voice, he stepped closer. 'Your brother? Who is he?'

'His name is Edwin. Edwin of Claverham.' Hearing his small exclamation she lifted her face hopefully. 'Do you know him, sir?'

'No,' the reply came at once, quenching her hopes. 'It would not be possible to recall the name of every man in the army. Which lord does he serve?'

'I—I don't know. He ran away to join the King. He's not yet sixteen.' Exhaustion, coupled with the realisation of the problems before her, made tears well hot in her eyes. 'Oh, sir, I must find him. I must take him home with me. Without him, Earl Torquil will claim my father's lands and there is no way I can prevent it.'

Sobbing, she laid her head in her hands and gave way to her misery.

Her companion said something, very quietly, but it was a moment before his words penetrated her despair and then they cleared her mind miraculously. For what he said was, 'Are you the Lady Judith?'

She lifted her head, looking up at his shadowed face in startled bewilderment. 'I am,' she breathed. 'How did you know? You *do* know my brother! Has some harm befallen him? Sir, is he—' Unthinkingly, she laid her hand on his chest, on the white cross of St John that glowed ghost-like against his dark tunic; then, recalling his status, she withdrew and curled her fingers in a ball at her throat. 'I'm sorry. I forgot that— But if you have news of my brother please tell me. I must know whether he still lives.'

'I do not know your brother,' he replied. 'To my knowledge I have never laid eyes on him.'

'Then how did you know my name?'

'My father mentioned it, in a letter he wrote to me.' Giving her a moment to digest this information, he added evenly, 'I believe you and I are betrothed, Lady Judith.'

She caught her breath, staring through the darkness in an effort to see the expression that accompanied his toneless voice, but all she could see was the glimmer of his eyes in the shadows.

'You—' she managed hoarsely. 'You—are—'

'Geoffrey de Belgarde, younger son of Earl Torquil of Brecon,' he supplied in that same even tone, and reached for her arm again. 'Come. It grows late. We must be indoors before curfew rings.'

CHAPTER
TWO

TORMENTED by aching limbs, a pain in her foot, and a hard hand clasped with unnecessary force round her arm, Judith was hustled through the dark streets of Acre. She was so tired that nothing made sense to her any more. That Geoffrey de Belgarde should be here, wearing the white cross which openly proclaimed him a soldier-monk, and that he could still claim her as his betrothed, when she had refused the offer of marriage— it was beyond comprehension. A hundred questions crowded in her mind but she was too breathless to ask them, even if she had been able to express them in coherent form.

The way back to the square seemed a great deal further than she remembered, and soon Judith saw a huge wall rearing ahead, with towers standing black against the stars. She was being forced towards a gateway at the foot of the wall, where armoured soldiers passed in and out by the light of torches.

'Where are you taking me?' she gasped.

'Where you will be safe,' he replied shortly. 'You know nothing of this land and, as you have already discovered, many dangers await the unwary. You were a fool ever to embark on this quest, but no doubt reckless-ness is a family trait.'

This sally made Judith come to a halt, forcing Geoffrey to stop, too. 'I go no further until you tell me what you intend to do with me!'

'God's teeth, but you have a suspicious mind,' was his weary reply. 'We are going to the King's own residence, the citadel of Acre. King Richard is absent, but the Queen is there, and other ladies. I trust you can make yourself useful to them in the short time before you depart—on the next ship to leave this port.'

'I shall not leave without Edwin!' she said fiercely.

She heard him take a breath as if to calm his exasperation and when he spoke he was so close to her that his breath fanned her cheek. 'I shall myself look for your brother. As your betrothed, it appears to be my duty.'

'You are not my betrothed!' she got out in a voice that shook. 'I refused the offer. I would beg in the streets before I would marry a de Belgarde. I know your purpose, sir. If you find my brother you will make sure he does not survive.'

The fingers round her arm clasped bruisingly tight, making her cry out in pain as he growled, 'You know nothing of me, yet you accuse me—'

'You are your father's son!'

'God's eyes!' he got out between his teeth. 'If you were a man—'

'If I had been a man, many things would be different,' she replied, quaking under the force of the anger she could sense in his powerful frame, transmitted through the brutal grip on her arm. 'And if you were a true knight of St John you would not swear so, or bully a helpless woman. You shame your holy vows.'

'Vows?' His hand relaxed a little and he glanced down

at his clothing as if he had forgotten the cross blazoned there. 'You display your ignorance, my lady,' he said. 'I took no vows, except to serve the order of St John for two years, as a confrère—a lay brother. I am free to marry if I please.'

A little breath almost of relief escaped her, but she retorted, 'Then you shall not marry me, sir. I will take the veil rather than give myself to one of the Earl's evil brood. That much I *can* deny him.'

'If you seek to wound me,' Geoffrey said in a voice charged with cold anger, 'your darts miss their mark. I have no wish to marry you. I shall choose my own bride, and she will not be a thoughtless wench who would risk her virtue by wandering unescorted in a strange town, nor ragged and dirty, nor sharp-tongued and full of hatred.'

Allowing her no time to reply, he forced her towards the gate of the citadel, where guards barred their way until Geoffrey announced his name. He hurried her across the courtyard beyond, where men and horses jostled prior to retiring for the night, and all but pushed her up the castle steps and into a great hall filled with servants who were mostly engaged in unrolling their pallets and blankets.

A steward came hurrying to ask their business, but, recognising Geoffrey, bowed low and called him by name—which surprised Judith, since there were many knights in the town and she had not expected the King's steward to pick out Geoffrey de Belgarde from the rest. She chanced a glance at her escort's face and was rewarded by a brief, irritable look from green eyes flecked with gold, fringed by luxuriant dark lashes.

'I have brought this lady to seek the Queen's protection,' he informed the steward, who gave Judith a disapproving stare and replied that the Queen was in the bower with her ladies.

'But if you intend to visit her,' he added, 'you must leave your sword with me, Sir Geoffrey. Those are the King's orders and I durst not disobey him even for you.'

Impatiently, Geoffrey concurred, handing his sword hilt-first to the man before half-dragging Judith towards the stairs that circled up a corner turret.

'I cannot be brought to the Queen this way!' she protested.

He paused and looked her up and down, making Judith freshly conscious of her dirty, bedraggled state. 'You have no choice, I fear.'

'You are cruel, sir!' she cried. 'You treat me ill.'

'I make no claim to be a courtier,' he replied. 'I'm just a soldier, already saddled with duties enough without the extra responsibilities you have forced upon me. If I seem rough, it is no more than you should expect.'

'Especially from a de Belgarde!' she shot at him.

His lip curled slightly and his eyes flashed a warning, but his only reply was to move on, taking her up the stairs and along a passageway where he knocked softly at a door and waited. By the light of a wick fluttering in a small bowl of oil, Judith considered his hard profile and told herself she hated and feared him. Geoffrey was as ruthless as his father. Yet when she had first seen him in the crypt she had thought him so fine. If only he had not been a de Belgarde!

The door came open, revealing a lady in a loose robe,

her tawny hair flowing about her shoulders and her face haughty with surprise and disdain. Instantly, Geoffrey released Judith's arm and swept a low bow.

'Lady Joan. Pardon this intrusion.'

Her eyebrows lifted a fraction. 'Sir Geoffrey? Is there news of the King?'

'No, my lady. Forgive me, but I came across this young woman—Judith of Claverham—lost in the streets. Her companions have deserted her and it seems hardly fitting for her to be left to sleep among the other pilgrims. May I leave her in your keeping until I can arrange a passage home for her?'

Joan of Sicily, sister to King Richard, looked Judith over with evident distaste. 'Lost in the streets, you say? Oh, very well, Sir Geoffrey, leave her with us. She may provide a diversion, I suppose. God knows we are all fretting in the absence of the King. And you can hardly keep her in your quarters, though I trust you will not burden us with too many of your lights o' love.'

Geoffrey stretched his lips in semblance of a smile, but his glance told Judith he would not soon forgive her for causing him this embarrassment. 'Your wit is keen as ever, my lady,' he murmured. 'I thank you.'

Making another bow, he turned on his heel and strode away without a backward glance, much to Judith's dismay. She felt deserted. For all his abruptness he was a link with home and Edwin, while the ladies' bower in the citadel of Acre was yet another place where Judith did not belong. That much was evident by the way Lady Joan looked down her nose as she opened the door wider.

What had she meant about 'lights o' love' Judith

wondered. Was Geoffrey de Belgarde in the habit of finding stray ladies in the streets?

In the soft flicker of rushlights, she saw a long room with its shutters open to let in the cool evening breeze and the sighing of the sea. Several curtained beds stood round the walls, and three ladies were gatherd round a fourth, who sat having her hair combed. All of them paused to stare and exclaim over Judith's dishevellment, though they were more sympathetic than Lady Joan. Judith was particularly touched by the kind concern of the seated girl—a young woman not much older than herself, with a rather plain face and lank, mousy hair— the Lady Berengaria of Navarre, Queen of England.

That night Judith lay in bed in the bower, clean again and wearing a fresh night-gown which had been found for her, but her mind remained as disturbed as ever. It was strange to hear the wash of waves outside, and the tramp of feet on the stairs as the watch changed at midnight. The very air smelt alien with the salt-tang of the sea and rich spices, plus the overpowering scent of the sweet perfume beloved by the Lady Sybil. Judith found herself longing for the familiarity of Claverham, or even the Priory. When she set sail from England she had not dreamed of the difficulties she faced, and yet despite it all something in her nature was stimulated by the challenge ahead.

Geoffrey de Belgarde had promised to find Edwin—if she could believe his word. The Queen herself, having heard Judith's story, had promised to speak with the King about it as soon as he returned from the siege of Darum, but still Judith lay awake worrying about her brother and planning to find him herself if the oppor-

tunity arose. Her mind strayed, too, to memories of
Geoffrey de Belgarde. What manner of man was he?
Soldier or monk; honourable knight or blackest villain?
He had threatened to find a ship to take her home. When
would she see him again?

For several days Judith remained in the bower, helping
the ladies dress their hair and embroider bright silks. She
was given fresh clothes and accepted as a lady-in-
waiting—and waiting was exactly her fate, waiting for
she knew not what. When she enquired if anyone could
say how long it would be before Geoffrey de Belgarde
returned, the Lady Joan snorted and said:

'We are not privy to the affairs of menfolk, mistress
Judith. Sir Geoffrey is off about his duties for the King, I
don't doubt, and has forgotten you. Best do as we all do,
and contain yourself in patience.'

Patience, however, was a quality the Lady Joan lacked; her restlessness affected everyone. Queen Berengaria, young, gentle and rather bewildered, was the
most forbearing, particularly after the cavalier treat-
ment she had received from the King. Taken to Sicily to
meet him, she had then been obliged to take ship for
Cyprus, where Richard had conquered the island before
pausing to marry his betrothed, after which he had
brought her on Crusade. Since then, he had been almost
constantly away from her, laying sieges or giving battle
to the Saracens.

Having heard this story from the cynical Lady Joan,
Judith wondered at the young Queen's fortitude, but
Berengaria never complained. She seemed happy in the

bower with her ladies, joining in their games and conversations and smiling over their tales of lords who came a-wooing.

Lady Joan, who was a widow, often railed loud and long against her brother the King and all men who abandoned their ladies for the sake of war, even in such a noble cause as the conquest of the Holy Land. Judith often found herself in agreement. She, too, was waiting for news of, or from, Geoffrey de Belgarde, and she became as impatient as Lady Joan.

It was the King's sister who devised the plan for an adventure. One morning she produced voluminous black robes and veils such as the Arab women wore, and announced her intention of taking a walk about the town in this disguise.

'Joan, you cannot!' the Queen gasped.

'Indeed I can,' came the crisp reply. 'Other Frankish ladies have adopted the fashion, why should we not follow suit? Shut up here day after day I am like to die of boredom. I am going. Who dares to come with me?'

'Not I,' Berengaria declared. 'The King would never forgive me.'

'The King need not know,' Joan retorted. 'If we slip out, no one will take note. Arab servants come and go in this garb.'

'I'll come,' Lady Sybil offered. 'I shall buy some new perfume in the souk.'

Smiling wickedly, Lady Joan rounded on the others. 'Matilda? Elena? And you, Judith? Mayhap you'll catch sight of your Sir Geoffrey—maybe with another lady. Imagine what fun you'll have with him if that occurs!'

'Geoffrey de Belgarde is no concern of mine, as I have

told you many times, my lady,' Judith replied, wondering why she found this manner of teasing so upsetting. 'But I will go, if the Queen allows it.'

'Only take care!' Berengaria pleaded.

Matilda and Elena elected to remain behind with the Queen, but the other three made their plans and stole out one by one, with Judith in the vanguard to test the efficacy of the disguise. The black robe, and the black veil round her head, concealed everything but her blue eyes, and the business of the castle so absorbed its residents that few even noticed the 'Arab' woman as Judith crossed the courtyard and went out by the postern gate, onto a hillside overlooking the harbour.

At the foot of the pathway she waited for Lady Joan and Lady Sybil to join her and eventually they arrived together, laughing at the success of their plan. All they sought was an hour's freedom, but for Judith the excursion was more than a prank. She hoped to find some clue to Edwin's whereabouts.

The three ladies joined the throng in the busy streets and made their way to the bazaar, where Lady Sybil set about her search for more of the sweet, cloying perfume she adored. To Judith's surprise, she heard other swathed women speaking in her own language— obviously Lady Joan had been right and Crusader ladies enjoyed the anonymity of veiled faces. For some of them it meant greater ease in conducting their love affairs while their lords were absent.

Across a mound of melons, Judith caught sight of young Tom, her urchin companion from the ship. Gone was his grey robe and in its place he wore a clean tunic, seeming to be on some errand or other as he strutted importantly through the crowd. She tried to catch his eye and, realising he would not recognise her in her disguise, went after him, past a half-naked black slave wearing golden earrings and fat merchants clad in silks and turbans. But just as she was about to call out to Tom she stopped dead, staring in total astonishment at a huge man who stood watching the sights—a man with long red hair and beard, wearing the mud-coloured tunic and stockings of an English peasant, a wicked long knife and a cudgel thrust into his belt. A man she had known since childhood!

'Magnus,' she breathed, her surprise turning to unbounded joy. 'Magnus! Magnus!'

This last cry made the man turn to search the crowd with furrowed brow as Judith pushed through a group of women and ran towards the red-haired giant, hardly knowing whether to laugh or cry.

'Magnus!' she said again.

'Aye, lady,' he replied in a puzzled fashion.

Judith threw the veil from her face and saw his ice-blue eyes widen in shock as the serf from Claverham recognised her.

'Mistress! How come you here?'

'How? Why, on a ship across the sea.' Delight made her laugh aloud. 'Did you come with Edwin? Oh, I should have known you would not let him come alone. Faithful Magnus! Where is my brother? Is he well?'

With a worried glance around the bazaar, he beckoned her into the shelter of a cart piled with skins. 'Aye, mistress, he's well, or was this morning when I saw him last.'

'This morning?' she repeated, her eyes shining. All

this time Edwin had been so near. 'Is he here—in Acre?'

'He was. He rode out with a guard that was taking a party of pilgrims to the shrines at Nazareth.' Still struggling to believe that she stood before him, he scratched at his tangled red hair. 'But, mistress, you shouldn't be here.'

'Everyone tells me that!' she cried. 'I had to come, to find Edwin. Even since the Earl told me he had run away I have been afraid for my brother.'

'The Earl,' he said with a frown, and spat on the ground in disgust. 'It was him that drove master Edwin to come. Your brother was miserable at Castle Belgarde. The Earl used him as his butt—used him cruelly and then taunted him for a coward, until my master thought of nothing but following the King. I've been with him every step of the way, and would be with him now if it wasn't for this.'

He nodded at the ground and Judith saw his foot was wrapped in bloody bandages. 'You've been hurt?'

'In a skirmish. It's nothing. I'd have gone to Nazareth, but the captain of the guard forbade me. I hate for the master to be out of my sight.'

'Will they be back today?' she asked.

'Nay, mistress, I know not. There was talk of them going further, perhaps as far as the Sea of Galilee. With the King keeping the enemy busy further south it's quiet at the moment, and the Saracens often let pilgrims pass unharmed. It may be a few days before they return.' Frowning, he shook his shaggy head and stroked his beard. 'But I'm not happy with master Edwin out of my sight.'

Neither was Judith happy. Another few days seemed an endless time now that she was so close to completing her quest. She laid a hand on the serf's brawny wrist, her face lifted in entreaty. 'How long have they been gone? Let us go after them. Can you borrow horses? Magnus, I must be sure that my brother is safe!'

It took a deal more argument, but her pleas and his own anxiety for Edwin made him agree, eventually, to find horses and meet her again.

As Judith paced impatiently, she suddenly saw Tom again, coming directly towards her. The lad's face lit up when he saw her and he told her he had been given a job of running errands for the garrison serjeants.

'You've done well,' Judith approved with a smile. 'Will you take a message for me? Go to the citadel and ask the commander to tell the Queen that I am safe. I am going after my brother, who is gone to Nazareth. Beg the Queen's pardon for me, but say I did not come here to sit in a tower. When I return I shall go to her and explain— she will understand, I feel sure.'

Tom swelled with self-importance, thrilled to be trusted with a message for the Queen herself, and darted away intent on carrying out the task without delay. He ran across the path of a group of mounted knights, and Judith held her veil across her face as she saw that they wore the insignia of St John. From her eye corner she searched their faces, but Geoffrey de Belgarde was not one of their number, which was a relief yet, puzzlingly, a disappointment, too.

After a while Magnus returned leading two horses. They walked towards the gates in the outer wall, quitting the town without trouble since the guards were occupied sorting out a camel-train laden with packs.

Beyond the wall a village of tents had blossomed beneath the palm trees and the hills stretched away, covered in low scrub and stands of cedar. Judith and Magnus took the road into the hills, and she rejoiced in the familiar feel of the animal beneath her as it cantered along, making her robe billow behind. This was the freedom she had so longed for while at the Priory and her heart sang as she contemplated her long-awaited reunion with Edwin. They would go home together and thwart Earl Torquil's plans.

As they left the coast behind, the sun seemed to grow hotter and the hills shimmered beneath a sky of hurtful blue. Soon Judith's clothes were sticking to her and she began to long for a drink.

'How far ahead will they be?' she asked as they slowed their pace to rest the horses.

The serf squinted up at the sky. 'One hour. Maybe more. We shall catch them before they reach Nazareth, unless . . .' His voice broke off on an indrawn gasp of alarm and Judith, following his gaze, saw three robed horsemen plunging down a slope towards them.

'Bedouin!' Magnus said under his breath. 'Brigands, mistress! Spur up. I'll keep to the rear and protect you.'

'I shan't leave you,' she protested.

His answer was a ferocious glare. He leaned to slap her mount soundly on the rump, making the animal leap forward with a bound that almost tossed her from the saddle. She glimpsed the Bedouin racing towards her, whooping and yelling, with Magnus riding to head them off, then a stand of trees took them from view. She hung grimly on, her head bent low over the horse's flying mane. With thumping heart and a mouth gone dry she watched the sere landscape flash by. The horse was out of control. It carried her away from the dusty road, over a hill and through a valley. Judith pulled at the reins but the horse only reared, danced, trying to unseat her, then thudded to earth and galloped on wildly, taking her further into unknown terrain.

At the brow of another hill she saw a green plain ahead, backed by craggy mountains that danced through a haze. The horse plunged down the decline as if scenting water, its hide flecked with sweat, and she let it have its head, thinking that soon it must slow down or die from exhaustion.

They thundered across the rich grasslands, scattering sheep, then abruptly the ground became wet and Judith was carried into the heart of hot, steamy marshland where tiny flies came buzzing round in clouds. At last the horse stopped, bending its head to drink from a pool, and Judith slid from the saddle, her knees buckling so that she almost fell.

Sinking down beside the pool, she threw off her veil and cooled her face with the water before taking a drink. It tasted a little brackish and tepid, but to her it was as good as sweet wine.

She realised that her gown was wet where she knelt. The entire earth was damp beneath its lush growth of plants. Leaping to her feet, she remounted and looked around. Mountains loomed ahead and behind, rugged sun-baked peaks lifting towards the sky. She knew she must reach higher ground or risk being bogged down in the marshes, but the nearest safe point looked to be ahead, not back the way she had come.

Of Magnus there was no sign. Despairingly she thought that Geoffrey de Belgarde had been right to call her a reckless fool. Now she was lost, and her rashness might have cost the faithful Magnus his life. Even if he had survived his encounter with the Bedouin he would not know where to find her. Her only hope was to try to get back to Acre.

She urged the horse to a walk and it obeyed, its flesh quivering and its tail flicking at the swarms of annoying flies. If she could find the coast then she would find Acre, or some other town, but her only guide was the sun. No human life moved in all that marshy wilderness. Only a snake glided through the grass, and a bird of prey floated high above.

The sun reached its zenith and still Judith rode across the marshes, sweat pouring from her to soak her thin chemise and gown beneath the robe which she dared not take off. She moved slowly, needing to watch every step, desperately keeping her fear at bay and forgetting the passage of time. At last the lush, dangerous green began to give way to rocks and firm ground, and when she looked up she saw foothills not far away, leading on to looming mountains where shadows lengthened as the sun slipped to the west.

The coast was to the west, she thought. To the west.

In a rocky valley she came across a stream where she stopped to drink and let the horse rest and crop some of the grass. Thankful to have crossed the marsh, she stretched out on the ground with an arm across her eyes, intending to ease her aching muscles for a while. Sleep took her unawares.

She woke with a start, hearing voices not far away—

male voices using an unknown tongue. The sun stood
low in the sky, edging behind the hills. Looking round
for the horse, Judith sat up in alarm as she saw that it had
gone. She might have wept had she not been more
concerned about the approaching voices. Their owners
sounded to be just behind a shoulder of hillside covered
in low cedar scrub.

Scrambling to her feet she ran for the deep shadow
thrown by the stunted trees and threw herself down
there, covering herself with the black robe and veil.
There she lay, and waited.

The men sounded to be in cheerful mood, chatting
among themselves and laughing in that melodious, liquid language of theirs. Their voices began to recede,
and Judith let out a sigh of relief, but a scuffling nearby
made her look up to see a rabbit dart from cover in the
hillside. A second later an ominous winged shadow
dropped like a stone. The rabbit squealed once then lay
still, and the hawk sat there, staring at Judith with
unblinking eyes.

She, too, remained still, praying that her luck might
hold. The hawk wore bells and bright ribbons round its
legs, so it was not wild. Those men must be out hunting.

A shrill whistle confirmed her guess. The hawk took to
the air in reply, to return to its master, and a moment
later a dog appeared to retrieve the kill.

Take it! Judith prayed silently, but the dog stopped,
alerted by her presence, and lifted its head to bark
sharply, the sound making her wince with despair.

Hidden by the hillside, one of the men shouted and
the others laughed as if deriding the dog's disobedience.
Judith, lying immobile with terror, heard a small patter

of stones and a moment later glimpsed flowing robes caught with a vivid scarlet sash in which was thrust a sword. She pressed her face to the ground, hoping that the shadows concealed her, but the man let out an exclamation and his hand came on her shoulder.

Cold with fear, Judith lifted her veiled head and saw a bearded brown face—a young, handsome face—surmounted by a turban. A gold earring dangled from one ear and black eyes danced with laughter as he slowly reached for her veil and unwrapped it, catching his breath at the sight of her silver-fair hair.

His teeth showed white behind the beard as he smiled broadly and said, 'Lady, you are far from home.'

Startled by his use of her own language, Judith pushed herself to her knees hopefully. 'Are you a friend? A Christian?'

'No, by Allah!' He laughed and sprang to his feet, calling to his friends, and three horsemen appeared over the rise of ground, Saracens all from their dress, two turbanned and one wearing a banded headdress with the end drawn across his face as if he disliked the dust.

The first man lifted one of Judith's fair braids, saying, 'Al-Khatun,' and adding, with a smile for her, 'I name you al-Khatun—Lady of the Moon, beautiful one. And I claim you as my prize.'

Horrified, Judith backed away, hearing one of the other men say something sharp and dismissive. There followed a bewildering exchange between the man who had found her and the man with his face covered. Both seemed annoyed and growing angrier with every word. Then the second man leapt lithely from his horse and came striding towards her, his robe flowing round long legs. As Judith cowered away he caught her arm in a firm hand.

Something about that grip on her arm made her look up at him. She could see only his eyes, glowering at her from the shadow thrown by the headdress—lynx-eyes, with furious golden specks sparking over green depths.

'God's wounds!' Geoffrey de Belgarde said under his breath. 'Can you never stay where you belong?'

Unable to believe her senses, Judith stared at him. His eyes seemed to pierce her through a growing mist, a roaring sounded in her ears, and she sagged against him insensible.

CHAPTER
THREE

As soon as she woke, she knew she was in an alien place from the scent of incense which came faintly in the darkness. Moonlight slanted through a wide latticed window beyond which there was a glimpse of trees swaying, and not far away water bubbled, as if a stream ran nearby.

Stirring, Judith discovered herself to be naked between cool sheets of finest linen, and she almost jumped out of her skin when a hand came on her forehead—a feminine hand, as she realised thankfully when the woman spoke softly. In a foreign tongue! With a sinking heart, Judith realised she was a captive of the Saracens.

'I don't understand,' she said, shrinking back from the shadowed figure which bent over her. The woman moved away to a corner, where light flickered as she adjusted a lamp, turning it up so that its glimmer showed Judith the outlines of strangely-carved chests and a chair made of some peculiar light wood.

The woman's skin was black, she saw. She wore a loose tunic and baggy pantaloons pulled tight round her ankles. Her feet were bare. Bowing, she made for the round-topped door, said something more, and departed.

Seeing the Arab cover-all lying across the end of the bed, Judith swiftly wrapped it round herself as she got up and moved silently to the door, listening a moment before trying the latch. As she had feared, the door was locked.

Trying to get her bearings, she moved barefoot to the window and peered out across a moonlit courtyard surrounded by low buildings, with light showing behind other latticed windows. A breeze came gently to fan her face through the opening. There appeared to be covered walks around the courtyard, and in the centre a garden with shrubs and trees grew round a man-made pool where a little waterfall splashed down—a thing Judith had never seen before and scarcely believed. Were the Saracens sorcerers to make water obey them?

Then a sound outside the door made her whirl round in apprehension. She clutched the black robe round her as Geoffrey de Belgarde came in, a stranger in his outlandish costume of shirt and loose trousers tucked into calf-high boots, a striped robe on top fastened with a wide silken sash. He had removed his headdress and this time there was no doubting his identity. She stared at him, bewildered and dismayed.

'So you've recovered,' he said brusquely. 'Perhaps now you will agree that I spoke the truth when I told you Outremer holds many dangers. This is not England, my lady.'

Holding the robe securely round her she watched him with wide, worried eyes. 'Nor is it Outremer,' she said in a low voice. 'This is no Crusader city.'

'That's true. When you crossed the plain of Esdraelon you entered enemy territory.' Throwing out an exasperated hand, he exclaimed, 'Why did you leave Acre? I told you I would return.'

'It was not you I sought!' she cried. 'My brother had gone to Nazareth, so I—I set out to follow him.' Even to her own ears it sounded a foolish exploit and her temper rose in readiness to answer Geoffrey's scorn. 'Did you expect me to wait forever without news?'

'Five days is hardly forever,' he replied, his mouth grim. 'But there seems little point in going over what is past. You are here now—though I swear I never believed a woman could be so vexatious. You repudiate my protection, yet you constantly seek it.'

'Not from choice,' Judith said bitterly. 'Fate has twice now thrown me into your path, but there will be no third time, sir. When I find my brother, we shall leave this land.'

His frown deepened, as if he could not believe her naïvety. 'You appear to think you will be set free. And escorted back to the Queen, no doubt. My lady, you have much to learn.'

'You cannot keep me here!' she protested, taking a step towards him and stopping as she realised that her movement caused the robe to part, revealing a glimpse of naked flesh that drew his glance. Angrily, she swathed herself more firmly, her face burning. 'I have no clothes. Where are they?'

'Burned, I suppose. The Saracens prize cleanliness highly and you were in a disgraceful state. Covered in dried mud, dusty, perspiring—'

'Through no fault of my own! Must you remind me? Oh, why have you brought me here?' She sank down on the floor, the robe settling around her as she laid her head in her hands. 'I do not understand what is happening. Am I a prisoner?'

'You will not be allowed to wander freely,' he replied. 'What would you have had me do? I was obliged to bring you here.'

She threw back her head to glare at him. 'And where is here? Where are we?'

'The fortress city of Megiddo. It guards a pass through the mountains.'

'An enemy stronghold!'

He shrugged, as if she remarked on the obvious. 'It was fortunate for you that I was with Prince Hasan when he found you.'

'Traitor!' she shot at him, leaping to her feet again. 'Every word you speak confirms it. Traitor to your King and your God!'

He glowered at her beneath frowning brows. 'Be careful what you say, my lady.'

'I will not! You are a friend of the enemies of Christendom!'

As Geoffrey moved towards her she backed away, but caught her foot in the hem of the robe and dragged it from one shoulder. Clutching at it, not daring to move in case she pulled it further, she hung there, forced to endure the slow scrutiny of his gaze as it travelled, with the intimacy of a caress, from her face to her throat and across her bare shoulder. She heard his breathing quicken and a shiver ran through her as she realised how helpless she was, with no protection but the loose robe whose voluminous folds seemed to have a will of their own.

'Traitor!' she muttered again, bringing his glance back

to her face. His lips tightened and his hand spread against her throat, a long thumb keeping her chin tilted as he stared at her with eyes glowing dangerously in his tanned face.

'I have learned to respect the Turks,' he said in a voice that was low with contained anger. 'Their leader is perhaps the most honourable man I know. But what does a woman know of honour? You will learn to control your tongue while you are here in Megiddo. Otherwise you may regret it.'

She wished he would stop touching her, for her flesh burned beneath his palm and she was unable to move, fearing that she might stumble in the robe that clung round her feet. 'I shall say what I please,' she got out hoarsely. 'But who will listen to a prisoner in a dungeon? Is that to be my fate?'

Almost absentmindedly, he stroked the tender skin beneath her chin while he considered her face with ironic eyes. 'No dungeon for you, lady. This room has been lent for your use during your stay. The Saracens understand that a man may wish to be alone with his wife at times.'

Uncontrollable shivers seized her. She felt cold now, and afraid, croaking, 'Wife?'

'I told them we were wed,' he said in an undertone, and bent as if drawn by invisible strings to taste her trembling mouth, holding her face so that she could not twist away. His free hand came round her, inexorably drawing her nearer, and Judith cursed the robe that hampered her hands, though she squirmed in his grasp. The hard muscles of an athletic male body through soft clothing shocked her as she experienced such contact for the first time and felt her own senses respond, despite the resistance in her mind.

His lips moved across her cheek, to her ear and the sensitive place beneath as he held her with a growing hunger her instinct understood.

'We are not wed!' she breathed desperately. 'You must not—'

'Must not?' He looked down at her with burning eyes deep as the sea, gold-flecked over slumbrous green depths. 'My lady, I shall do with you as I please. Do you not understand? I had to tell them we were wed, or Prince Hasan would have claimed you and placed you in his harem. I said you had come in search of me, foolish and passionate child that you are. The Saracens understand such things. You should be grateful to me.'

With a whirl of desperate effort, she pushed at him, lifted the robe to free her feet and wrenched away, swathing herself securely once more.

'Grateful?' she cried. 'Were it not for your father I would not be here; my brother would be safe, and perhaps my father would be alive. If you expect gratitude for treachery and humiliation then seek elsewhere, sir. The Saracens may understand such things, but I do not!'

He moved as if to reach for her again and Judith stiffened defiantly, her untidy braids pale against the enveloping black robe. Geoffrey's lustful mood turned to scorn.

'Faith, but you weary me,' he said. 'Very well, I shall do as you suggest and seek elsewhere. Sleep well, my lady.'

Turning on his heel, he strode out, leaving Judith to shiver alone and wonder what the morrow would bring. She heard the key turn in the lock, and when she ran to the door she found it secure. She was, indeed, a prisoner.

She lay in bed between the silver moonlight and the golden lamplight, cold to her soul with fear. In a Saracen stronghold she could hope to find no friend. There was only Geoffrey and he had proved to be as treacherous as his father, in league with the enemy. Was he giving them secrets of King Richard's movements, or the numbers of each garrison? Everything in her cried out against the truth which Geoffrey himself had not denied, and she thought again of the first time she had seen him, in the Crypt of St John—a knight with eyes that had made her aware of her womanhood, so tall and fine with the white cross blazoned proudly on his tunic. How could he be so base and faithless?

But even in Turkish dress he had still looked fine, arrogantly male with that air of vital strength. Without willing it she remembered how his body had felt and how his mouth had melted with hers. She shuddered with revulsion at the memory—except that she was no longer sure that it was revulsion she had experienced. The upheaval of all her senses was a feeling for which she had no name, but she fancied there had been pleasure mixed in with it and she flushed with shame. She must not allow such a thing to happen again.

Geoffrey de Belgarde was in league with the enemy. Why else would he have been hunting with them? Why else would his 'wife' be treated so kindly? Locked up she might be, but it was a pleasant room, not at all like the dark dungeons where she had imagined the Saracens kept their prisoners.

Eventually she must have slept for she woke to find the room bright with sunlight and the slave-woman coming in bringing a breakfast of fruit, goat's cheese and some kind of flat bread-cake. She thanked the black-skinned woman and was rewarded with a smile and a flow of unintelligible Turkish, which included some pointing to the slave's own full bosom with repeated use of the word 'Zenobi'. Judith gathered this was the woman's name, though it told her little. Clearly there was no way she could ask questions.

After a while, Zenobi returned and made signs to Judith to follow her. Closely wrapped in the robe, she cautiously peered out of the door into an airy tiled passageway, where the woman beckoned her on.

Along the passage, archways gave access to the court-yard, where marble steps led down to the pool and a group of brightly-dressed women chattered happily, their laughter coming clear in the sunlight. Beyond, they crossed an ante-room and came into another big room, tiled all in marble, where a deep bathing pool had been sunk in the floor, its water gently steaming. Towels lay on benches, with pots of unguent and scented oils in ornate bottles. By signs, Zenobi indicated that Judith was to take off her robe and step into the pool.

She glanced nervously around but they appeared to be alone and beaded curtains across the far doorway provided a reasonable veil. Besides, hadn't she heard that the Turks kept their women apart, in separate quarters? Surely no man would venture here. She disrobed and climbed carefully into the bath.

After a while her nervousness vanished and she began to enjoy the warm, scented water. Zenobi knelt on the side, smiling and chattering as she poured more oil and helped Judith wash her hair. How delicious it was to feel really clean again!

Her hands ran sensuously across her body, to her throat and shoulders, her blue eyes darkening as she recalled Geoffrey de Belgarde's brown fingers against her skin. Had he really gone to find comfort with some other woman? she wondered with a strange contraction in her stomach. A Saracen woman?

After the bath, she sat on one of the benches wrapped in a towel while Zenobi dried her hair, and she knew she must not allow herself to be influenced by the luxuries of Saracen living. They were Infidels, enemies, barbarians who sought to throw the Christian armies back into the sea, and if Geoffrey had turned traitor she would not follow his example.

Alerted by the clicking of the bead curtain, she looked up to see a slender girl approaching, dressed in silk trousers and short-sleeved top heavy with embroidery beneath a gauzy coat that floated as the girl walked. Gold bangles clinked on her arms and around one ankle, their glitter emphasising the lustre of dusky skin. Hair as black as a starless night hung about her shoulders in shining locks, and she had some black kohl round her eyes to emphasise their shape and gleaming sloe-colour. Judith could see that the girl was extraordinarily beautiful, though she could only recently have reached mature, marriageable age. She looked to be, at the most, fourteen. She also looked distinctly unfriendly.

'You are Judith,' the girl said in heavily-accented

English. She lowered herself sinuously to sit on the bench, staring assessingly into Judith's face. 'My name is Mariamne. I am sister to Prince Hasan.'

Made wary by the watchful look in narrowed black eyes, Judith said, 'You speak English very well.'

'Yes.' Mariamne tossed a lock of raven hair from one shoulder. 'My brother taught me—and the lord el-Asad.' She glanced at Judith sidelong as if expecting some reaction to this. 'Have you enjoyed your bath?'

'Very much,' Judith replied. 'In my country there is nothing like this. Where does the water come from?'

Mariamne's eyes widened. 'From springs in the mountains, of course. It is heated by fires on its way to the pool. Water runs to every house through—through conduits, as the lord el-Asad calls them.' Again she looked through her lashes as she spoke the name, mystifying Judith.

'Well, I wish we had them in England,' she said with a sigh. 'Every drop of water there has to be drawn from a well, or a river.'

'So the lord el-Asad told me. It is a good name for him—el-Asad. The Mountain Lion. Do you agree? He reminds me of a panther, in the way he moves. But it is his eyes, like a great dangerous cat. Except when he smiles. Then I think that if I stroked him he might purr.'

Judith felt suddenly chilled, every hair on her body standing on end. The man in question could be no one but Geoffrey de Belgarde and she was astounded to hear such ideas from the lips of one so young.

'Did he not tell you of me?' the girl asked, wide-eyed. 'We have been friends for many months, since first he came with my brother to visit the Sultan. He is a beautiful man. He will make beautiful sons for you.'

Flushing hotly beneath the towel, Judith remembered that she was supposed to be married to Geoffrey de Belgarde. But to think of bearing his children made her sweat.

'Does this embarrass you?' Mariamne asked, looking with interest at the colour flooding Judith's cheeks. 'But it is the reason for marriage. A man needs sons.'

'Are you married?' Judith asked, attempting to change the subject as Zenobi drew a comb through her long hair.

Mariamne shrugged prettily. 'A suitable man has not been found. I am in no hurry. I enjoy myself. I enjoy learning English with the lord el-Asad.'

'Yes, I expect he enjoys that, too,' Judith said, imagining sourly how those lessons must progress. The Saracens, she had heard, had strange ideas about relationships between the sexes. A man could take more than one wife and have as many concubines as he chose. Presumably Geoffrey had slipped into the immoral ways of his friends. A chill settled on her as she guessed which woman Geoffrey must have gone to after he left her the previous night. She regarded the beautiful Turkish girl with fresh eyes, experiencing an uncomfortable pang almost like jealousy.

Toying with the bangles on her wrist, Mariamne said. 'Is it true that Christians take only one wife?'

'Perhaps you should ask the lord el-Asad,' Judith replied bitterly.

'I did so, last night. He said it was true. But if the one wife cannot give him sons, what does he do?'

'He prays for strength to endure his misfortune!' Restless, she waved Zenobi and her comb away and stood up to pace the tiles. It was humiliating to be so taunted by this dusky Saracen child.

'Is there no method of divorce?' Mariamne enquired archly.

'Yes, there is, if circumstances allow. But a man who loves his wife would not set her aside easily.'

'Does el-Asad love you?' The question came with a gleaming sidelong look.

Judith stopped her pacing, not knowing how to answer, and Mariamne leapt to her feet, her fingers curled into claws as she spat, 'He does not! I know this. He loves *me*. And I shall have him. He will become a Muslim and take me to wife—when he has divorced you, pale one!'

'He will not need to divorce me!' Judith snapped, and was instantly sorry for the indiscretion as Mariamne became still, her expression questioning and hopeful.

'You are not his wife?' she said under her breath, her face alight. 'You are not! This is wonderful news.'

'It still does not mean he will marry you!'

'But he will. I shall ask my uncle the Sultan to give him to me, to seal the peace that el-Asad is seeking. Oh! Hasan will be delighted.'

Alarmed, Judith stood tensely, wondering what mischief she had started. 'Hasan? Your brother? He wants you to marry Geoffrey?'

'He wants *you*!' Mariamne said with a little laugh of pure triumph. 'He was much taken by his Lady of the Moon—he named you for your hair—al-Khatun. It displeased him to find you were married to el-Asad.

Now I can take the frown from his face. Oh, do not look afraid. My brother is a rich and handsome man—a nephew of the Sultan. And he is . . . you call it virile, I think. Yes, virile. Passionate. Lusty. You will be his favourite concubine.'

Leaving Judith speechless with consternation, she danced away and disappeared through the bead curtain.

She was taken back to her room and Zenobi brought her a set of clothes, which Judith gathered had been sent to her by Mariamne. Despite her dislike of the odd costume, she allowed herself to be dressed in the baggy silk trousers with beaded ankle bands, and a matching beaded jacket which fitted closely to her figure but, to her discomfort, left the top curves of her breasts bare. The clothes felt strange, but were a lovely sky-blue, and certainly better than the black robe.

But nothing could still the anxious flutter of her heart. She was imprisoned in the room with only her thoughts for companions, though she could hear the laughter of other women in the courtyard. How stupid she had been to say she was not married to Geoffrey. Now the 'virile' Hasan might try to claim her, and heaven knew what would ensue.

She wondered under what conditions Mariamne had learned those words which she had spoken with such relish—passionate, lusty. Judith herself hardly knew the exact meaning of those terms, but she could guess. They meant the way Geoffrey de Belgarde had been the previous night. Did he behave like that with Mariamne?

She paced the room, her hands clenched, wanting to scream and thinking that if Geoffrey came she would attack him for being so dishonourable. Truly he was a son of his evil father. How she hated and despised him!

One phrase of Mariamne's puzzled her—'the peace that el-Asad is seeking.' What did it mean?

But he wouldn't let Hasan take her, would he? She would die before she became the mistress of an Infidel, however handsome and powerful he might be.

Hearing the key turn, she swung towards the door expecting to see Zenobi again, but it was Geoffrey de Belgarde who strode in, his face made even darker by angry blood as he slammed the door shut behind him.

'You fool!' he began, and stopped as he noticed the way she was dressed, his lynx-eyes widening as his glance flicked over her. But the look vanished as soon as it appeared, leaving him frowning. Two strides brought him to stand before her and he grasped her shoulders, shaking her mercilessly, growling at her, 'I told you to guard your tongue! What made you say we were not wed?'

As the motion stopped, Judith stared at him breathlessly, her head whirling and a strand of silver-gold hair veiling her eyes. 'It was the truth!' she cried, furious with his rough handling of her.

'Aye, but there is a time for truth and a time for lies, as you would know were you not so empty-headed.' He pushed her away from him with such force that she fell across the bed and lay there on her side, watching as he strode to stare out of the lattice at the courtyard.

'How did you find out?' she asked in a small voice.

'Hasan told me,' he said over his shoulder. 'Lady, you try my patience every time we meet! Do you never pause to consider before you act or speak?'

'I did not mean to say it,' she muttered. 'Besides, you should be pleased, since it is Mariamne you care for.'

He swung round, frowning, 'What?'

'Nothing.' Faced with that fierce-panther stare she dare not repeat the sally, though she wondered why the thought of his loving Mariamne should be so unwelcome to her.

Impatiently, he came to sit on the opposite side of the bed, leaning towards her with an expression so angry she feared he might use more violence. 'You little fool! Do you know what you have done?'

'I know well enough,' she said dully. 'I knew as soon as the words had been said, but it was too late to take them back. Geoffrey . . . you will not—not let Hasan take me, will you?'

He appeared not to understand, for his frown deepened momentarily. Then he leapt to his feet with a bitter laugh. 'Hasan may take you, for ought I care. Aye, take you and put you in his harem, with the rest of his collection. That is not what concerns me.'

She sat up, feeling as though he had slapped her, and tears choked her voice. 'Then why are you angry? If you care nothing for my welfare—why did you claim to be my husband?'

'Out of a misplaced sense of chivalry,' he growled. 'Which I bitterly regret. Were I able to turn back the hours I would deny all acquaintance with you, lady. You have been a thorn in my side since the moment we met, and now with one word you have ruined the work of many months.'

Realising that there were matters of which she had no knowledge, she made no reply, only sat unhappily watching his grim face and taut-held frame as he strode restlessly to the window and back, fixing her with a look of loathing.

'You named me traitor, Lady Judith. I thought to allow you to believe what you pleased, so perhaps the fault is mine. But you were wrong. King Richard knows I am here. King Richard sent me here—on a personal mission of peace.'

'To befriend the enemy?' Judith said in disbelief.

'The Saracens are a people worthy of friendship!' he exclaimed, throwing out an arm. 'The Sultan Salah-ed-Din is the most honourable man I know—a civilised man. And the Saracens are doughty warriors, defending what they believe is right. We respect them for that.'

'But you fight them!'

'We fight for the return of the Holy places into Christian hands. But after a battle is won or lost then envoys come and go. The Sultan has a great respect for King Richard. When the King is ill with the recurring fever that plagues him, the Sultan sends him fruit, and sherbet—which only the Turks know how to prepare. Then again they confront each other on the field. This is how wars are waged among civilised men.'

'It seems a strange way to me,' Judith said dully. 'Enemies turned friends, only to become enemies again as the occasion suits.'

Geoffrey frowned impatiently. 'I do not ask you to understand. Women know nothing of these things. It is to do with honour. And I fear that the Sultan Salah-ed-Din is the most honourable of all. He has never broken a treaty, nor given his word lightly.'

She stared at him incredulously. 'How can you speak thus of the leader of our enemies?'

'I speak the truth! I am proud to be an ambassador to his court.'

'Is he here?' she asked in a hushed voice. 'In this city?'

'At present, yes. He has come to escape the heat of Jerusalem, and I am under his protection. Or was.'

'Was?' Apprehension made her throat dry. 'What do you mean?'

'I mean that your stupidity may prove costly!' he replied in harsh tones. 'It has taken me long hours of talk, many days of travelling back and forth, and months of waiting, to persuade the Sultan to trust me. I go among his people without weapons, to display my trust in them. And at last I had succeeded. The Sultan listened to me, and I had made a friend of his nephew Prince Hasan. Forgive me if I seem unaffected by your future of cosseting among Hasan's favourites, but you seem not to understand—You have proved me a liar, impugned my honour . . . I may pay for this dearly!'

The words struck Judith with the force of lightning, but before she could speak there came a tramp of feet in the passage. The door slammed open, crashing back against the wall, and the room seemed to swarm with yellow-clad men brandishing weapons.

Even as Judith sprang to her feet in alarm, two of the soldiers made straight for Geoffrey, fastened their hands on him and dragged him away.

CHAPTER
FOUR

In a fever of anxiety and fear, Judith stood with her fingers twined in the lattice of the window, staring out at the pleasant, peaceful courtyard and wishing she could speak the language of the women who were relaxing out there. They laughed together, and ate figs and grapes, the happy scene seeming almost a blasphemy when Geoffrey . . . Dear God, what would the Turks do to Geoffrey because of her?

When the door opened she turned swiftly, but her visitor was only Zenobi, bringing a tray of food. How did one ask after the welfare of a prisoner of the Sultan?

'El-Asad—' she began feverishly. 'Is he safe? He—' But she shook her head in despair when Zenobi lifted her hands and shrugged, clearly not knowing what she was trying to say.

Sighing, she sat down and tried to eat, but the food had no appeal for her. If anything happened to Geoffrey she would be to blame. She would spend the rest of her life with an unbearable guilt and sorrow.

The Mountain Lion, she thought with a bleak smile. It was an appropriate name for him since he moved with the lazy grace of a cat and exuded a sense of contained power. He did not deserve punishment because of one small lie he had told—told to save her, what was more.

But perhaps Mariamne would intercede for him. Yes, of course she would. The thought was a small comfort.

Zenobi reappeared to collect the tray and exclaimed over the untouched food, but Judith waved her away. Then just as the slave turned to the door it swung open and a richly-dressed, bearded Turk strode in, carrying himself with such proud arrogance that his presence seemed to fill the room. Zenobi gasped and prostrated herself, while Judith stood up, awed by the regal figure and fearing the news he might bring. He clicked his fingers at the slave and evidently ordered her to leave, for she departed with a worried glance at Judith.

The visitor smiled, performed a graceful bow and said, 'Lady of the Moon!'

She knew him then—Prince Hasan, the man who had discovered her on the hillside. Quivering like a cornered fawn, Judith stood quite still, her eyes deep violet pools in her pale face.

He was a handsome man, she thought, and his smile came easily—too easily. He wore a pointed turban and an expensive brocade surcoat swept to his knees, hiding most of the linen trousers he had tucked into his boots. At his waist a green sash held a curved knife in a jewelled sheath, but it was his face which gained her attention, for there she hoped to read her fate—and Geoffrey's. All she could see, however, was a neat black beard, smooth brown skin and deep-set eyes like sparkling jet. He looked pleased with himself.

'What have you done with Geoffrey?' she got out through stiff lips.

'I?' he laughed. 'I have done nothing with him. It was my uncle who ordered his arrest.'

'Your uncle—the Sultan?'

Hasan's eyes danced with amusement as he declaimed, 'El-Melik en Nasir al Sultan Salah-ed-Din, Yusuf ibn Ayyub—known to you unpoetic Franks as Saladin. Yes, I have the honour to be his nephew. Are you worried about el-Asad, sweet Lady of the Moon?'

Judith hesitated, wondering how best to reply. Hasan seemed friendly, but beneath his surface smiles there lay a Saracen heart and mind which she could not hope to comprehend.

'A woman should not worry,' he said, coming softly towards her. 'It spoils her beauty.'

Nervous of him, Judith straightened her back. 'I have heard that in your country a man does not enter a lady's room when she is alone. You should not be here, my lord.'

'But in your country such things are done,' he replied with a smile. 'Many strange things take place in the land of the Franks, if I may believe all I hear.'

'I'm not French!' she said tensely. 'I'm English.'

Laughing softly, he advanced again and lifted a hand to touch her cheek. 'English, French, Germans—they are all the same to us—all Franks—all Crusaders—all enemies.'

'Except for Geoffrey de Belgarde. He said you were his friend. Help him, my lord. Please help him.'

'For you I would do much,' he said with a sorrowful shake of his turbanned head. 'But this is out of my hands. Al Sultan Sulah-ed-Din will decide his fate.'

'But the Sultan would listen to you,' she said desperately. 'Or—or perhaps to your sister.'

Swift anger furrowed his brow. 'My sister is not concerned with the fate of Infidels!'

'No,' she faltered. 'No, of course not. I did not mean—'

Thoughtfully, Hasan lifted a lock of her hair and surveyed it with covetous eyes. 'Al-Khatun. I named you well. Your hair is like moonlight. Your skin,' he touched her face again, 'like finest ivory. You shall lie against silk pillows and I shall adore you, for you have given my enemy into my hands.'

She caught her breath at the sudden hardness in his voice, and flinched away from his touch.

'I have long mistrusted him,' Hasan said, 'but my uncle was misled by his fair words and seeming honour. Yet now we know him for a liar. A man who will lie in small things may also lie in great things. Do not concern yourself for his fate. It will be quick and clean. A sword—so!'

He made a sudden chopping motion with his hand, making Judith wince and close her eyes as if to shut out the horror. But her mind showed her the picture all too clearly—Geoffrey kneeling, his hands tied behind his back, his head bent, and the sword sweeping down—

'No!' she cried, and fell to her own knees, clasping her hands to plead with him. 'I beg you, my lord . . .' Searching her mind for some way of escape she decided on a desperate gamble. 'He—he did not lie. It was I who spoke in haste. Your sister misunderstood me.'

Hasan drew a breath of disbelief and stepped away from her, his eyes narrowing. 'He is your husband?'

'He is—he is my betrothed. Promised to me in marriage. My husband-to-be.' Praying that he would understand the subtleties of this assertion, she saw him frown and stroke his beard.

'We shall see who speaks the truth,' he said softly. 'Dry your eyes, al-Khatun. El-Asad still owns his head. But you may yet live to enjoy my harem and provide me with a favourite son.'

Once more Judith found herself alone in that room she had come to hate. She wept bitterly against the bed, her hair a silver waterfall flowing onto the blue beaded jacket as she prayed with all her heart that she and Geoffrey might escape from their peril. Whatever he might be, she could not bear to think of him slain by a Saracen sword.

After an endless time when she was by turns hopeful and distraught, she heard the soft thud of several pairs of feet in the passageway. One of the yellow-robed guards appeared with Zenobi, who made haste to drape Judith in her black Arab robe and veil before indicating that she must go with the guard.

Feeling that nothing could be worse than being alone in that room, she ventured into the corridor and found several more guards waiting. They marched either side of her, along tiled ways and down steps, through cool, airy rooms and up more steps, and at last into a silk-hung throne room humming with people. All fell silent as she appeared. Most of them were bearded Turks, clad in flowing robes, their eyes turned to watch as she was led in. She glimpsed Geoffrey standing surrounded by guards, though his head was high. Then a hand in her back urged her on, to the foot of the steps which led to the throne. The handsome, richly-clad Hasan stood on the steps, while seated on cushions, cross-legged, the

Sultan Salah-ed-Din himself looked down at her with thoughtful eyes.

Judith had always pictured this chief of enemies as a demon, but to her surprise he was a mere mortal, a thin-faced, slightly-built man, black-bearded and be-jewelled. A ruby gleamed in his turban, with other gems on his fingers and round his throat, where she glimpsed a white scar above the collar of his scarlet tunic. Around him the guards in their saffron uniforms stood with drawn swords, alert for any trouble. Above the throne hung bright green banners embroidered with the golden Crescent of Islam.

In the Sultan's face Judith read weariness —perhaps even illness—but his eyes seemed kind. A little ray of hope lightened her spirits; then the next second she was sprawling across the steps, the imprint of a hand still hard in her back. Lifting herself, she looked up imploringly at the man who could bring instant death to any who displeased him.

'Rise up, Judith,' the Sultan Saladin said quietly. 'Rise up, and remove your veil.'

With fear-stiffened muscles, she pushed herself erect and unlooped the veil, letting her hair stream about her shoulders.

Glancing at Hasan, the Sultan remarked, 'You spoke truth, my nephew. She is fair. Now, Judith, I wish you to perform a task for me.'

He reached into his tunic and brought out a parchment, which he handed to Hasan, who passed it gravely to her. Unrolling it in bewilderment, Judith glanced at the message.

'I speak a little of your language,' the Sultan said. 'But

I do not read it. Tell me what it says, child.'

She scanned the page, swallowing the gasp that almost escaped her when she saw what it was—the letter Earl Torquil had written to inform his son of his betrothal to her. He had written as though the matter were already settled. Had Geoffrey used this letter to prove his point?

She chanced a glance at him and met his unwavering gaze across the room. It seemed to encourage her.

'Read it aloud!' the Sultan commanded.

She did so, haltingly at first, not changing a single word since she was sure the Sultan already knew exactly what it said. This was a test she had to pass if she wished to save Geoffrey's life, for she guessed that he had had the same idea as she. To the Saracens a betrothal was as sacred as a marriage and, had they been betrothed, Geoffrey's use of the word 'wife' might be justified. She was almost grateful to Earl Torquil for having taken her agreement for granted.

'So,' the Sultan said as she came to the end of the letter. 'Is this the truth?'

She lifted frank blue eyes to his face. 'Yes, my lord.'

At this, Hasan broke into a torrent of Turkish which his uncle stilled with a gesture, his gaze fastened on Judith's white countenance.

'You came in search of the knight Geoffrey?' he asked. 'You came to marry him?'

With an effort, Judith kept her face still and her eyes calm. 'Yes, my lord.'

'Then you are his wife, but for the ceremony of marriage?'

'I am.'

'Good.' The Sultan seemed relieved, but Judith heard

Hasan draw a rasping breath and when she glanced at him she saw his eyes narrowed in anger. A moment later Saladin was issuing orders, making some of his guards bow and quit the room while a murmur of interest and amusement ran through the waiting courtiers. One of the tall, yellow-robed soldiers touched Judith's arm and motioned her to join Geoffrey. She backed away from the throne, wondering if she could believe the Sultan's benevolent smile.

Geoffrey appeared to be relaxed, though his hands were lashed together in front of him and those bright lynx-eyes flashed coldly at her as she paused beside him. Even so, she was glad of his presence in a room full of enemies.

'What is happening?' she breathed. 'Did I do right?'

'It is always right to speak the truth,' he replied in an equally low voice, his glance warning her to guard her tongue.

'And now?' she asked. 'Will they set you free?'

'I believe so, when the ceremony is over.'

'Ceremony?'

A wry smile touched his lips as he regarded her upturned face and let his gaze rest for a moment on the soft curves of flesh exposed at the neck of her robe. 'The Sultan has sent for a Christian priest who is among his captives. We shall be wed, Lady Judith, to prove the truth of what we have said. Fortunate for us that it *was* the truth, eh?'

A breath caught in her throat and she threw up a hand as if to guard her lips from letting out an exclamation, but she caught herself in time and spread her fingers as a veil for her exposed bosom. The look in his eyes made her feel hot, suddenly aware of her femininity, but there was cool mockery, too, which annoyed her. This man—the man she had sworn never to marry—would become her husband here in this alien place, and there was nothing she could do to prevent it without risking both their lives.

Shortly, the guards returned, bringing with them a cringeing figure in a long grey robe, the top of his tonsured head shiny with sweat. Evidently he had not been told the meaning of this summons to the Sultan's presence, for when he was flung down at the foot of the steps he huddled there, clutching the simple wooden crucifix which hung at his girdle and muttering prayers in Latin.

The Sultan made a sign and a soldier bent to drag the priest to his feet, his eyes full of terror as he glanced round the room.

'Calm yourself,' Hasan said impatiently. 'You are needed to perform a wedding ceremony.'

'Here?' the man croaked.

'Here,' Hasan agreed, and signalled Geoffrey and Judith forward.

The sight of them made the priest's eyes threaten to leap from his head, for what he saw was a clean-shaven man in Turkish robes accompanied by a slender girl enveloped in black, with hair as fair as moonlight on gold.

'We are Christians,' Geoffrey said drily. 'Never fear, you will not be punished—here, or hereafter.'

A movement drew Judith's eyes to Hasan, who stepped forward drawing his wickedly-curved knife and paused to glance at her with fathomless dark eyes. 'Do I release him, or cut his throat?' he murmured.

'Release him,' she said at once, her hands instinctively clasping round Geoffrey's arm as if to prove that she was his. She did not know why she had made the gesture but she felt it to be right and the contact with Geoffrey's firm warmth beneath his sleeve calmed her unsteady heart-beat.

She watched as the sharp blade slid through the bonds that bound his wrists and Hasan lifted his eyes to his rival's face. For a second the two stared at each other in silence, then Hasan made an angry gesture and returned to his place on the steps beneath the throne.

'You wish to be wed?' the priest said in a shaking voice. 'You are both agreeable?'

'I am,' said Geoffrey.

'And I,' Judith managed through the catch in her throat. She had started to tremble as if she had the ague until her 'betrothed' turned to her, taking both her hands in his own while the priest muttered in rapid Latin.

Aware that Geoffrey's gaze was on her face, she could not look at him but kept her eyes on the strings that tied his shirt at the base of his brown throat. She felt the warmth of his hands as he held her firmly, in a way that might have been meant to reassure her, though she could not help but feel that he was afraid she might let him down at this last moment. How ironic it was—she had said she would sooner marry a serpent than any de Belgarde, but here she stood allowing herself to be tied to Earl Torquil's son.

The priest made the sign of the Cross beside them and

said, 'It is done. You are man and wife before God, even in this heathen place.'

'We are grateful,' Geoffrey said, a long finger tilting Judith's chin as he bent to brush his lips across hers and smiled a smile that did not reach his eyes.

A murmuring among the crowd reminded Judith of their audience and she heard the Sultan speak, addressing Geoffrey as 'el-Asad'. In reply Geoffrey bowed low and said quietly to Judith, 'You will be returned to your room. The Sultan and I have things to discuss.'

'But—' Her protest died as he turned away and the guards came round her, to escort her away from the throne room.

She spent the rest of the day alone in her chamber wondering what was happening to Geoffrey. Had the marriage ceremony convinced the Sultan of his trustworthiness?

As twilight brought lamps to flicker in the rooms across the courtyard, Zenobi reappeared bringing a light for Judith—a strange-shaped bronze lamp like a flattened jug with a wick protruding from the spout. Smiling, the slave made signs for Judith to follow her and, wondering what lay in store now, Judith obeyed.

Once again she was escorted to the bathing room, where she was bathed, oiled and perfumed before being returned to her chamber. Zenobi brought a gown of pink muslin scattered with sequins and, despite Judith's protests, helped her out of the blue trousers and jacket and dressed her in the gown, all the time talking excitedly, with many a coy glance at Judith's face.

Realising that she was being prepared for her bridegroom, Judith felt sick. The muslin was as opaque as mist, revealing more than it concealed. Even if she had been willingly married, such a garment would have made her blush, but in the circumstances it was indecent. She had no desire to be Geoffrey de Belgarde's wife. He had married her only to save his own head; she knew well enough he did not care for her.

After Zenobi had gone, Judith sat on the bed wondering how she could rebuff Geoffrey. But perhaps he would not come. After all, he knew as well as she that the marriage had been a travesty, and if he were a gentleman he would not take advantage of it. But Geoffrey, as he had already proved, was no gentle knight to take pity on a lady's helplessness.

She climbed beneath the sheet, which at least provided more adequate covering. If she were asleep, perhaps he would leave her alone. But no sooner had she lain down than she heard the key turn. The door opened, and Geoffrey was there, a long silk robe flying open to reveal that all he wore beneath was a pair of loose trousers.

'So tired, dear wife?' he said tightly, approaching the bed.

She sat up, clutching the sheet to her throat. 'Stay away from me, sir.'

'That may prove difficult,' he replied. 'It is expected that I sleep here tonight. The door is being watched. If I leave, the Sultan may think it odd.'

'Then you may sleep on the floor!'

'I would do so, were I not in need of a good night's rest. And we may be spied upon. It would look strange if I preferred a hard floor to my marriage bed on my wedding night—especially when you were so anxious to wed me that you hastened all the way from England and then risked your life to ride after me into enemy territory.'

'You know that is not true!'

'*I* know it, but it is what the Saracens believe. We must play out this piece of mummery to its end.' He threw off the silk robe so that the lamplight played across his well-muscled chest and shoulders. 'Come, make room for me. And never fear—I shall not molest you.'

'Even if I believed that I would not let you near!' she gasped. 'Stay away, sir!'

For answer he turned away, blew out the lamp and, to her utter dismay, paused to remove his remaining garment before lifting the sheet. She threw herself the other way, leaping from the bed into diamond-patterned moonlight that streamed bright through the lattice while Geoffrey, apparently determined to sleep in the bed, spread the sheet tidily over him and lay down.

'Is this the way a true knight behaves?' she cried.

'My lady,' his voice came softly through the dimness, 'your gown is transparent as cobweb. You will be cold.'

'Sooner cold than ravished!' she retorted, but she moved into the shadows where he could not see her so clearly. She wished the moon would go behind clouds for its brightness filled the room and she could see Geoffrey lounging on one elbow, his head in his hand as he watched her.

'This coyness is out of place,' he said irritably. 'I have promised not to touch you if you lie with me. Come, be sensible. The night air is chill in these mountains.'

'I would not sleep next to you if you were fully-clothed

and bound hand and foot,' she declared. 'As it is, you are naked and I—'

'And you are next-to-naked, as I can see.'

Horrified, she attempted to cover herself with slender arms, but her efforts only made Geoffrey say sardonically, 'Why hide yourself? You are beautiful, my lady. And I am your husband. Aye,' his voice became thoughtful, 'that is true. And though I am a knight of St John I took no vow of chastity.'

In one lithe movement he threw back the sheet and left the bed, making her close her eyes after one brief glimpse of his naked frame. She felt his hands on her shoulders, touching her hair before he cupped her face between his palms, lifting it to his as he bent to kiss her with sensuous thoroughness.

Judith dared not move. The knowledge of his nakedness brought heat to flood all her veins and if she fought him she would be obliged to touch his bare flesh.

'Neither of us chose to wed, my lady,' he murmured against her ear. 'But the contract is accomplished. We both spoke our consent. Why not make the best of it? I have need of a woman.'

'Then go and buy one in the streets!' she hissed. 'One who will be flattered by the attentions of el-Asad, the Mountain Lion.'

His fingers bit into her shoulders suddenly, making her gasp with pain. 'Do not mock me, Judith. I take pride in the name given to me by the Sultan.'

'The Sultan? I thought it was your mistress who named you. Do you sharpen your claws on her, too?'

'Mistress?' he repeated, his voice ominously quiet.

'Aye, sir.' She flung back her head to face him in the

moonlight. 'But perhaps for her you purr, Mountain Lion. Did you purr last night?'

He swung her round, pinning her against the wall full in the silver light while he moved a little away and let his gaze devour the sight of her in the mist-fine gown. His breathing quickened and she sensed the desire in him as he growled, 'Nay, lady, but I shall purr tonight before I have done with you. The Mountain Lion needs a mate and if she prove a wild-cat so much the better.'

He dropped his head, imprisoning her mouth with his own, his hands moving behind her back, one to tangle in her hair while the other slid down her spine to press her close to him. Now it was Judith who used her claws, scoring her nails down his chest and attempting to batter at him with her fists; but her arms were almost useless in the strong bonds of his embrace and she felt herself weaken, her senses beginning to respond to his kisses.

She gasped as her body touched his and encountered his aroused state. Her hands slid across his ribs, making her aware of the warm fragrance that enveloped him and, of their own accord it seemed, her fingers began to explore the taut muscles in his back as her lips parted beneath his onslaught. The desire to fight ebbed further as her flesh discovered the pleasures of a man's nearness and her body melted against the urgency of his, starting fires inside her.

Lifting his head, he stared down at her with moon-dark eyes, easing the muslin robe from her shoulders so that it fell about her feet. She shivered, though whether from cold, fear or delight she could not tell, and a moan escaped her as he drew her fully against him, his hard muscles warm to her softness as he kissed her eyes, her ears, her throat.

'You shall be my wife in every way,' he said hoarsely. 'Do not deny me, Judith. I have need of a woman. Great need.'

The moonlight spangled through sudden hot tears that blinded her. She had begun to believe that his fierce passion was inspired by tender feelings, but his words mocked her romantic fancy. He needed a woman—any woman—and since she was available he would take her, with as much thought as he might pluck an apple from a tree.

He kissed her mouth again, plundering its sweetness while his hands ran over her in roughly intimate caresses, but she no longer felt the rising tide of desire. It had ebbed in disillusionment. She could not stem the tears that streamed down her face. Why did it have to be like this? Why could he not woo her gently, even if it was a lie?

Tossing her up into his arms, he carried her to the bed, laying her down and himself beside her, his mouth hot against her throat. She closed her eyes, feeling tears slide down her temples into her hair as she lay passive under his hands, no longer caring what happened.

Abruptly, he lifted himself, his face dark with an emotion that might have been anger. 'Do not weep!'

'What would you have me do?' she said brokenly. 'Laugh? Let not my tears affect you, sir. Abuse me if you must. Prove yourself a true son of your father. And if I hate you for it, do not ask me why.'

'God's blood!' he got out through his teeth—and glanced towards the lattice as a soft click sounded, his expression changing from black fury to alarm.

Judith caught her breath as she saw that the lattice had swung open. A slim figure sprang into the room, a feminine figure crying passionately, 'I shall not let her have you, el-Asad!'

'Princess!' Geoffrey leapt up, across the bed from the dark-skinned girl who darted forward on bare feet. She lifted her arm, and Judith saw the dull gleam of a knife as it plunged towards her, aimed at her heart.

CHAPTER
FIVE

EVEN as Judith twisted aside, Geoffrey threw himself across her and the downward thrust of the knife stopped as he caught Mariamne's arm. His weight threatened to stop Judith's breath, but she saw him wrest the knife from the girl's hand, gasping something in Turkish before he pushed Mariamne away and stood up, reaching for the silk robe to throw it about his lean nakedness.

Judith sat up, curled on the bed with the sheet clutched to her breast, her head whirling and her heart hammering. On the floor, Mariamne lay in the patterned moonlight, her long hair trailing round her across the carpet as she wept bitterly.

'What is this?' Geoffrey demanded, standing over the prostrate girl. 'Mariamne, are you mad?'

The reply was a flow of Turkish, incoherent with tears. She flung her arms round his ankles and kissed his feet, weeping and muttering.

'What is she saying?' Judith asked breathlessly.

He flung her a bitter look. 'Words for my ears, not yours. Mariamne—this is no way for a princess of the blood royal to behave. What would your brother say?'

A wail escaped the girl, as if she had forgotten her brother in her jealous rage. She came to her knees, clutching at Geoffrey, seeming to be pleading with him, her voice soft and full of a misery which might have touched Judith's heart had she not been the girl's intended victim. Her nerves were still jumping from the suddenness of the attack.

'Mariamne,' Geoffrey said in a consoling tone, but continued in Turkish so that Judith was left to guess what was said. All she could comprehend was the tone of their voices—he speaking softly, she begging, then grateful, her eyes lifted to his. Judith saw the adoration in the girl's face and wondered furiously just what Geoffrey was telling the Muslim princess. She did not recall his ever using that gentle tone with her. He sounded like a lover, she thought, and was herself filled with such passion that had the knife not been safely in his hand she might have used it on him.

With a gasp of sorrow, Mariamne clasped his hand, kissing it fervently, clinging to him when he tried to ease away. Finally she released him and fell once more to the floor, weeping.

Geoffrey glanced at Judith. 'Tell her you forgive her.'

'Tell her what?' she gasped in astonishment. 'She tried to—'

'She did not understand! Say she is forgiven.'

Tightening her mouth mutinously, she said with disgust, 'Aye, she is forgiven. I do not hold *her* to blame for this.'

'You will tell no one?'

'Whom should I tell?'

He spoke once more to Mariamne, bending to help her to her feet. She grasped his hand again, lifting it to her cheek while she looked up at him with mournful, adoring eyes. Then she turned away towards the window, to leave the way she had come, but before she closed the lattice she looked at Judith and Judith sensed a fierce hatred that chilled her.

She watched as Geoffrey checked the lattice, making sure it was firmly closed.

'Had I known it would open,' she said bitterly, 'I would have escaped before now.'

'Escaped to where?' he demanded, the robe rippling as he swung round, reminding her of the powerful body beneath it. 'No woman is allowed to leave the palace without escort. And had you managed to gain the streets beyond you would have been stopped. Fortunate for you that you did not attempt it.'

As he stopped to lay the knife on one of the chests an exclamation of pain escaped him and he paused to look at his forearm.

'What is it?' Judith asked anxiously.

'A cut. It is not deep, but it bleeds well.'

Concerned, she climbed from the bed, taking the sheet to wrap round her Roman-fashion, one end thrown over her shoulder. 'Let me see.'

In the moonlight the cut looked black, with dark smears running down to his hand. She began to search in the chests, cursing the lack of light, and eventually found a piece of linen from which she tore a strip to bind his wound. Throughout this operation Geoffrey remained silent, allowing her to tend him.

'So you do possess a few wifely skills,' he said sardonically when it was done.

'Aye, sir, but that is the limit of my willing co-operation. Am I likely to be attacked by any more of your lights o' love? I seem to remember the Lady Joan made some such comment, but I thought she was jesting. Apparently she knows more about your dalliances than I do.'

'How could she know about something which does not occur?' he asked in a hard voice.

Tossing back her hair to look at him in the grey light, she gave a bitter laugh. 'You deny it?'

'Assuredly I do.'

'You expect me to believe that Mariamne conceived her passion for you without encouragement?'

'Believe it or not, as you will. It is the truth.'

'Hah! You would not have said so had you heard the way she spoke of you. You have taught her English, have you not? And other kinds of lessons, unless I miss my guess.'

He caught her arm, whirling her against him, his free arm circling her waist as he growled, 'I have never been alone with her. Had I tried, it would have meant my death. The Saracens protect their women fiercely.'

'But if she were not so protected you would gladly have gone to her!' she accused. 'And she would have been all too willing to welcome you. Such a wondrous passion she has for you—she would stoop to murder in its cause.'

'The Turks have passionate natures and hot blood,' he said in a low, angry voice. 'And some of us Franks share that fieriness. We love the sun, not the cold and sterile moon, which waxes and wanes inconstantly.'

His words seemed to be proved by the heat emanating from him, threatening to envelop her in its seductive power as she felt his thigh hard against her. Infuriated by his insinuation that she was cold, she yet determined to resist him if he continued to make love to her. She wondered if she could reach the knife which lay not far away.

But a sudden commotion in the corridor startled them both. Voices shouted and feet pounded, approaching their door.

'Quickly!' Geoffrey breathed.

He picked her up and threw her on to the bed, dragging the sheet from around her. He placed himself half on top of her, his mouth on hers and his hands in her hair, just as the door was flung open.

Geoffrey lifted himself as if startled, drawing the crumpled sheet to cover Judith as he stared angrily at Hasan, who had burst in accompanied by several soldiers bearing flaming torches whose light bathed the scene in gold. Breathless and bewildered, Judith peered fearfully at the bearded emir.

'What is the meaning of this outrage?' Geoffrey roared, sliding from the bed to confront Hasan.

'Your pardon,' the emir said smoothly with a slight bow. 'I had not meant to interrupt your pleasure. We are seeking my sister the princess Mariamne, who is missing from her bed.'

'And did you think to find her here?' Geoffrey demanded.

Hasan's smile was cold and made his eyes glitter. 'Or you absent, el-Asad. I was mistaken. I beseech your pardon for this intrusion, but I was obliged to find out. My sister is a determined and wilful girl. I must make haste to find her a husband.'

'Your sister is no concern of mine,' Geoffrey said. 'I

have been here with my wife all night.' He laid slight emphasis on the word 'wife' and Hasan's dark eyes swept to Judith, considering her tousled state.

'You are a wise man,' he said. 'And a fortunate one. Sleep well. You will not be disturbed again.'

'Make sure we are not, my lord,' Geoffrey replied threateningly. 'Or the Sultan shall hear of it. I am an envoy of King Richard, and under the protection of Salah-ed-Din.'

Ordering his men out, Hasan bowed again and cast a lingering glance at Judith before he swept out, closing the door—and turning the key.

'Now you are a prisoner, too,' Judith breathed in the returned darkness, afraid of the hatred she had sensed in Hasan. 'He does not trust you.'

'He never trusted me entirely,' came the reply as he walked across to stare out of the window at the moonlit courtyard.

'But you said he was your friend.'

'Aye, but friendship between enemies is always tainted with distrust. He came here to remind me that I must not take one wrong step. He knew I would not be fool enough to meet Mariamne. Pray God she has returned to her room by now.'

'Are you concerned for her?' she asked.

'She is a foolish child.'

'But beautiful.'

He flung a bleak glance at her. 'I cannot disagree with that. Are you jealous, my lady?'

'I only wonder at your lack of discretion where she is concerned. There is something between you, and Hasan knows it. For a man who is on a mission of peace, such an association seems reckless.'

One stride brought him back to the bed, where he leaned over her, saying tautly, 'There is no association! There could never be, since she is a Muslim and I a Christian.'

Fancying she heard regret in his tone, Judith said acidly, 'And a knight of St John, dedicated to honour and valour. Which you seem to forget with great ease. Do your knightly vows mean nothing?'

'They mean far more to me than the vow I made today when I spoke my willingness to be wed,' he replied coldly.

'It was done to save your life!'

'Aye, and for your part it was done to save you from Hasan's harem. But one thing you misjudged—marriage to me will not preserve you from the cloistered life. I have no lands, no fortune, no means of supporting a wife.'

Incensed, she sat up, clutching the sheet across her breasts. 'You imply that I trapped you into this jest of a marriage? You set the trap yourself, sir! I want only to find my brother and take him safely home. Once he is secure in his inheritance I shall gladly retire to the Priory. I want nothing of you.'

His lips twisted as he stared at her, his dark-lashed eyes flickering across every feature of her face and resting at last on her lips, as if derisively to remind her that she had not entirely resisted his attentions. 'That is as well, since I have nothing to give you,' he said. 'My only possessions are my armour and my sword. But I shall use them to aid you in your quest. We shall find your brother.'

'How can we find him when we are imprisoned here?' she demanded.

'We are imprisoned only for tonight—and that because Hasan seeks to insult me. Tomorrow I return to the King with the Sultan's reply to his peace offer, and you shall go with me.'

Relieved, she asked, 'To Acre?'

'To wherever the King is. First I must see him, before I find your brother and put you on a ship bound for England.'

'It cannot be soon enough for me!'

'Nor for me.' He threw himself down on the bed, turning his back on her. 'Now sleep.'

Wondering why the thought of returning to England brought her no joy, Judith tucked the sheet more firmly round her and considered the tousled dark head on the pillow next to her. She could feel his warmth, and his weight on the bed beside her was a disturbing sensation.

Sleep seemed far away. She sensed that Geoffrey, too, was awake as the moon moved across the sky, leaving the room in darkness.

'Geoffrey?' she breathed.

'Aye,' he said irritably.

'If there is peace, will you return to England, too?'

'I had not planned to,' came the reply. 'I shall join a garrison somewhere. But peace will not come yet. The King and the Sultan are not serious in their negotiations. It is a game they play, to save face. Do you know what the King offered this time?'

'No.'

The bed swayed as he turned towards her, supporting his head on one hand. 'He offered the hand of the Lady

Joan in marriage to the Sultan's brother—both of them to rule in Jerusalem. It amused the Sultan, and his brother el-Adil. But they have agreed, to see what the King will do.'

Flattered to be informed of such secrets, Judith found her nerves were all alive to the nearness of the man who was now her husband. 'And what will he do?' she asked.

'He will duck,' Geoffrey said, his voice deep with dry humour. 'The Lady Joan has been known to throw missiles in her temper. She will never agree to such a marriage. She will be even more angry than you were when you found yourself wed to me.'

Something in his tone made a tremor run through her and she tensed herself, expecting him to reach for her. Instead, he turned his shoulder to her and said, 'Sleep now. We have a long journey to make tomorrow.'

He composed himself for sleep and lay still. After a while, Judith too turned on her side, curled into a ball with her back to him, the sheet held tightly round her as she wondered why she felt slighted.

She slept deeply, without dreams, and came slowly awake with a warm weight across her middle, which she discovered to be Geoffrey's arm. His head lay in the curve of her shoulder, his dark hair brushing her cheek and his breath fanning her skin. During the night, the sheet had slipped to her waist and his arm held it there.

For a moment she lay staring at the painted ceiling in the first glow of sunrise, painfully conscious of her naked breasts. But when she tried to pull the sheet up Geoffrey stirred and opened his eyes, the increased pressure of his arm prevented her from moving. Very slowly, he lifted his head and kissed her breasts softly, causing little ripples of delight to move through her as her body responded. But when he looked at her she saw the mocking gleam in his eye and swiftly covered herself.

'You were not so coy in your sleep,' he said softly. 'Do you not remember clinging to me?'

'No, I do not,' she replied in horror, hot blood rising to her cheeks. 'I would not!'

'No? But I remember it.'

'You were dreaming—and probably not of me.'

Smiling, he lifted himself to lean over her, pinning her shoulders with his arms while his hands played in the silver waterfall of her hair. 'It was no dream, lady. Almost you tempted me to take you as you slept. Be thankful that I contained myself. If it happens again I may not be so chivalrous.'

As she opened her mouth to make a sharp retort he kissed her, robbing her of breath as his lips moved slowly and deliberately on hers. One of her arms was pinned beneath his body, but she lifted the other intending to repulse him only to have her fingers disobey the moment they encountered the warm muscles beneath his silk robe. How firm and strong he was, she thought dazedly, scarcely realising that her mouth had softened under his and she was responding ardently to his kisses.

But her growing euphoria was interrupted by the entry of Zenobi, who affected not to notice the pair on the bed as she set a tray on one of the chests.

'A pity,' Geoffrey said under his breath. 'I could have wished our imprisonment to last a little longer.' Rolling over, he sat on the side of the bed and stretched himself with much the same indolence as the great cat for which the Turks had named him. 'I must see about arrangements for our journey. Eat a good breakfast. It may be hours before we reach another meal.'

Pausing only to draw on the trousers he had discarded the previous night, he strode out, sharply reminding Judith that she was nothing to him but a nuisance which must be borne until he found Edwin for her. Yes, he would have made love to her, but only to appease his appetite.

She found herself feeling cold and bitterly angry with her own body for having lulled her into enjoying his embrace. She felt rejected, too, for she was beginning to realise that she cared for Geoffrey de Belgarde in a way she had never expected.

Tended by Zenobi, she was bathed and perfumed, and then the slave appeared with an armful of clothing which Judith recognised as her own—the linen chemise and blue gown, her veil and circlet, even the black Arab robe. All had been cleaned and mended. It was good to be dressed in her own way again, dressed modestly in a ladylike fashion, but she watched with regret as Zenobi carried away the pink muslin gown. She possessed nothing so alluring—though of course she had no wish to be alluring for Geoffrey de Belgarde. In her own sensible clothes she would present less temptation to his barbaric male desires. For that she was glad. But she would have liked to own that muslin gown, if only to look at it now and then.

'We must leave,' Geoffrey said as he came in. 'Have you everything?'

She began to reply, but stopped in surprise as she saw that he, too, was garbed in Western dress—the black tunic with its white Cross and the black mantle similarly blazoned on the shoulder. Buckled round his waist he wore his scabbard-belt, but the sheath contained no sword.

'I brought nothing but the clothes I had on,' she said.

'And this.' Reaching into his tunic, he brought out her purse and tossed it to her, still clinking with gold. 'You may need it, since you married a poor knight. Come, our escort is waiting.'

Drawing the black robe around her, Judith fastened the purse at her girdle and followed him, thinking ruefully that a change of clothes had altered his character. Gone the passionate, hot-blooded man of the previous night, and the tender lover of only a short while before; now he was a soldier again, brusque and impatient. Why should she regret the metamorphosis?

At a side gate in the palace walls, a mounted escort of the Sultan's own saffron-robed guard, all armoured and heavily armed, waited for them. Judith was worried to see Hasan with them, astride a mettlesome black stallion and holding the reins of another, milk-white, horse.

'A gift from the Sultan for King Richard of the Lion's Heart,' he informed them. 'The Lady of the Moon may ride him.'

'Tell the Sultan that the King is honoured by his gift,' Geoffrey replied, linking his hands for Judith's foot. She leapt astride the horse and settled her skirts, honoured to be entrusted with such a beautiful animal, which was of Arab blood, lithe and fleet.

It appeared that Hasan intended to ride with them, for as Geoffrey mounted another spare horse on her left the Saracen Prince moved up on her right and the escort formed two lines behind, the leading riders holding billowing banners which bore the golden Crescent. They set off through streets paved with white stone, past low white houses, among dusky-skinned people who bowed to Hasan but stared at his companions with suspicion.

'My people do not trust Franks,' Hasan said with a tight smile that showed a glimpse of teeth behind his beard. 'Lady, I must apologise for my intrusion last night. I understand your lord's annoyance. I, too, would have been annoyed to be interrupted on my wedding night with such a beautiful wife.'

'I trust you found your sister safe and well,' Judith replied.

'We did. Forgive me for believing she might have been with el-Asad. It was a nonsense, of course. Why should he look at her when he has a wife like you?'

Because she is exotic, beautiful and has a passionate nature, she thought bitterly, recalling how Geoffrey had virtually accused her of being as cold as the moon. Compared to Mariamne she was a pale shadow from a Northern land. But Hasan regarded her with open admiration, which was balm to her injured pride.

'Even had I been free,' Geoffrey was saying, 'I would not have dared raise my eyes to the Princess Mariamne, as you well know, my lord. But, as you say, I was not free. My heart had long been in the hands of the Lady Judith.'

Hasan laughed. 'A delightful speech for a Frankish knight, el-Asad. You seem to have learned the essence of poetry. Perhaps we may yet make you civilised. And you, Lady of the Moon? Do you return this great love?'

'From the moment we met,' she said, and glanced at

Geoffrey to see him lift an eyebrow slightly, his eyes mocking her.

Beyond the heavily-guarded gateway in the stout walls, a panorama of mountain peaks opened up before them; stark rocky crags with little vegetation, with a twisting track running down to the pass over which the walled city stood guard. The heat of the day increased as they descended from the heights, at length reaching a greener valley where Hasan drew rein.

'This is where we must part,' he told Judith, regret in his eyes and voice. 'But if Allah wills it we shall meet again. I only pray I do not have to meet your husband in battle, for if I do I shall kill him with exquisite pleasure.'

'You may try,' Geoffrey said evenly.

Smiling slightly, Hasan reached inside his robe and drew out a golden glitter which proved to be a chain from which hung an opal, shining with rainbow lustre beneath the opaque white surface. He urged his horse nearer to Judith's and placed the chain round her neck, looking deep into her eyes. 'This is for you, in remembrance,' he said softly. 'A moonstone for the Lady of the Moon. Allah guard you, al-Khatun.'

Uncertainly, Judith glanced at her husband and found him glowering evilly, his jaw clenched as if he were having difficulty with his temper. Then she looked into Hasan's ardent eyes and said, 'I—I thank you, my lord,' her fingers stroking the smooth contours of the heavy gem.

Moving away, Hasan signalled to one of the guards, who presented Geoffrey with his sword. He held it for a moment, looking narrowly at Hasan as if wondering whether to run him through, then he slammed the weapon into its sheath.

'You are wise,' Hasan said with a smile, stroking his beard. 'My uncle and your King would not be pleased if we two diplomats should come to blows. But if we meet in battle it will be different, el-Asad. Farewell, my friends.'

Wheeling his horse so that it reared for a moment, his cloak billowing out behind him, Hasan rode away, back towards the fortress city, with the guards galloping behind. A cloud of dust rose to hide them as the thunder of their hooves diminished.

'You should not have accepted such a gift,' Geoffrey said roughly.

'Why not?' Judith asked in astonishment, though secretly she delighted in this display of jealousy. 'He meant it kindly. And if the King may accept a horse from the Sultan . . . Surely such things are a step towards peace.'

A muscle jumped in his jaw as he stared at her fingers caressing the jewel. 'Hasan meant it as an insult to me. Saracens do not give gifts to other men's wives, for fear of the husband's anger. He knew I was powerless to stop him. It was your place to refuse it.'

'Then you should have said so!' she retorted, snatching her hand down from the pendant. It was not jealousy that moved him, she realised, but wounded pride. 'Do not expect me to understand the subtleties of dealings with the Saracens. Do you wish me to throw it away?'

'No, keep it,' he growled. 'It will pay for your passage back to England.'

He spurred his horse and rode ahead, leaving Judith

to follow. Her mount galloped with graceful ease but her mouth was set and her eyes stormy as she told herself she would be only too happy to take ship and leave this impossible man behind. But in her heart she knew it was not true—the thought of leaving Geoffrey laid a great heaviness on her.

Around mid-morning they were joined by an escort of Knights Templar, proud warrior-monks wearing white surcoats marked with a red cross. The same emblem fluttered on the pennants of their lances and each man looked stern, bronzed by hot sun. It seemed that they had expected Geoffrey's return from Megiddo and had come to meet him, though their leader looked surprised to find a woman with him.

'My wife, the Lady Judith,' Geoffrey introduced her without further explanations. 'What news of the King?'

'He is at Ascalon,' the captain replied, 'awaiting your report with great impatience. The French armies grow restless. They mislike this talk of peace and would have the King ride on to Jerusalem without delay. If we make haste, we may reach his encampment before nightfall tomorrow, but it will mean hard riding.' He glanced doubtfully at Judith.

'My lady will not delay us,' Geoffrey replied, his tone telling Judith that he would brook no weakness on her part. His mind was set now on his duties and she was an encumbrance to him.

'Shall we pass by Acre?' she asked him. 'Since my brother is there—'

'Acre is to the north,' he replied brusquely. 'We ride

south. I shall leave you in the care of friends of mine at Jaffa, where you will be safe until I am free to seek your brother.'

They set out at a swift canter, leaving the mountains and coming to the fertile Plain of Sharon, where fields of flax and cool olive groves grew between the mountains to the east and the coastal sand-dunes of the west. At every waterhole they paused to allow the horses to drink and rest, and after noon, stopping at one of the chain of fortresses which guarded the land, they exchanged their mounts for fresh ones. The milk-white Arabian stallion was left to rest, with instructions that he be taken at a more gentle pace to the King.

As the sun went down they reached another Templar fortress, where makeshift arrangements were made to accommodate an unexpected lady. Judith spent an uncomfortable night in a blanket tent in a corner of the chapel, disturbed every few hours by the Templars' devotions. She was not sorry when Geoffrey came to wake her at dawn, though her muscles ached and a snatched breakfast gave little respite before their journey continued.

Once more they changed horses at a Crusader encampment around midday, but for the riders themselves there was little rest. Judith's thighs were stiff as wood. At home at Claverham she had ridden the manor with her father, but gently, and never for more than an hour or two. She longed for a rest, and some shade as a respite from the heat, but when they stopped it was only for a few minutes and she was obliged to force her tired limbs back into the saddle. She forbore to complain. She was aware that Geoffrey kept glancing at her, as if to check how she was faring—perhaps waiting for her to show how tired she was—but she gritted her teeth and kept grimly on, riding beside him.

Finally, as the shadows lengthened, they emerged from a group of low hills and came to a river lined with the green of eucalyptus trees. As the horses splashed across the ford, Judith saw a town ahead, with Crusader pennants flying from its towers. But closer at hand was a watering hole shaded by trees, where a camel train had gathered and tents stood in the cooling gold of the late sunlight.

'Wait here,' Geoffrey instructed the captain of his escort. 'I shall return shortly. Come, my lady.'

Too weary to reply, Judith obediently urged her mount on among the somnolent camels, down the dusty track between green fields and through the great gateway into the busy, white-walled streets of Jaffa. A strong citadel built on a mound reared its walls and towers against the sun, but Geoffrey led her past this castle, down a steep street beyond which she glimpsed the waters of the harbour. It reminded her of Acre. Acre was where she wanted to be, with Edwin, not all these miles away among strangers.

Geoffrey stopped at the gateway of a house not far from the harbour and dismounted, coming to help her down. He looked weary, too, his face streaked with dirt where dust had mingled with his sweat. As he held out his arms to her his eyes were expressionless, his mouth a grim line.

She all but fell into his embrace, so tired that her legs would hardly hold her, and for a moment she sagged weakly against him.

'You have done well,' he said gruffly. 'You did not disgrace me.'

A bitter laugh escaped her. 'Thank you, my lord. Not for anything would I disgrace you.'

She fancied that he bent his cheek to her hair, but then he straightened and she thought it must have been illusion, for he was unlikely to make such a tender gesture. There came a patter of sandalled feet and an enormously fat woman appeared in the gateway, beaming with delight as she threw out her hands.

'Sir Geoffrey! I told Zebulon he must be mistaken, but he swore it was you. And it is! Why, what is wrong? Is the lady ill?'

'No, Xenia. Just weary.' He sounded to be smiling but Judith could not lift her head to see. She leaned against his shoulder, staring at the woman who wore a shapeless gown of striped cotton gathered into a plaited-leather girdle. Dark hair was loosely braided and coiled about her ears, while her wrists were adorned with copper bracelets. Around her neck hung several chains of gold. Her bright smile revealed a missing tooth, and even though her eyes were almost lost in flesh they shone with motherly kindness.

'Weary?' she repeated. 'She's exhausted, poor child! Whoever is she?'

'The Lady Judith, from England. She's—my wife.'

The woman caught her breath in surprise. 'Wife? But I thought—Ah, listen to me chatter! Bring her inside. You both look as though you need some food and rest.'

With Geoffrey's arm supporting her, Judith managed to walk through the gateway into a cool courtyard with a red awning to protect it from the glare of the setting sun.

She saw a well, a donkey tethered beside a hay-manger, and a manservant who hurried to obey when the fat woman spoke to him in some strange language.

It was cooler still inside the house, where rich carpets lay on a mosaic floor and great jars stood in corners. Geoffrey led Judith to a low couch where she sank down gratefully, sighing with relief, as the manservant returned with a jug of wine and some silver goblets.

Judith sipped the rich liquid, feeling it soak into the parched corners of her mouth and throat as she wondered why Geoffrey did not sit down. As she stretched her aching neck to look up at him, he drained his goblet and set it on the low table by the couch, watched fondly by the fat woman.

'My thanks,' he said. 'That will see me through to Ascalon. Xenia, will you take care of my wife for me? She has money for—'

She cut him off with a wave of her hand. 'She is welcome in my house. But you are not leaving at once, surely?'

'I must. The King expects me.' He bent to take Judith's hand, lifting it to his lips, and his eyes met hers, heavy with solemnity. 'Farewell, my lady,' he said, and was gone.

She sat quite still, staring at the doorway as Xenia padded after him to make her own farewell. She could not believe he had gone so abruptly, leaving her to the care of a total stranger. Her hand still bore the imprint of his lips and she stared at it numbly, remembering that strange, sombre look in his eyes. Was he deserting her for ever?

But no. After he had seen the King he would come

back and they would find Edwin together and then . . .
Then she was not sure what would happen, nor did she
care to think about it too deeply.

CHAPTER
SIX

'WELL!' Xenia exclaimed as she returned. 'He was in a fine hurry, but then Sir Geoffrey takes his duties seriously. My dear, you need a rest. Come, let me take you to your room. I'll have one of the maids bring you water to wash away the dust, and later we'll have supper together, when you feel stronger.'

Feeling that she was no longer mistress of her fate, Judith followed her hostess out into the courtyard, where steps climbed to the upper storey, which boasted a balcony and two sleeping rooms.

'I'll send up some fruit, too,' Xenia said, leaving Judith in the cool dimness of a room with closed shutters, where only a tiny line of gold came from the setting sun to stripe across the floor and the narrow bed. A maid brought water and Judith washed herself, taking off everything but her shift as she lay down and closed her eyes, letting exhaustion carry her down into sleep.

When she woke the sun had gone. From the balcony she saw the flicker of lights in other houses, and on ships in the bay. Torches gleamed from the watch-towers of the great citadel which sat on its mound commanding the harbour, its high stone walls sweeping almost into the sea.

In the room downstairs, she took supper with Xenia,

tended by the man Zebulon and the two maidservants, all of whom were natives of this land of Palestine, so Xenia said. She herself was a Greek, from Byzantium, married to a wealthy merchant who was at present away on a trip down the Nile. They had no children.

'But I like to think,' Xenia added, 'that if I had had a son he would have been a man like Geoffrey de Belgarde. Sir Geoffrey saved my husband's life, you know. Demetrios was travelling overland with one of his camel-trains and Sir Geoffrey was captain of his escort of Hospitallers. They were attacked by a band of Saracens and Demetrios was wounded. I believe he would have died if Sir Geoffrey had not tended him. Since that time we have been friends. He visits us whenever he is in Jaffa.'

'Did he say how long he would be gone?' Judith asked.

Xenia shook her head sadly. 'How could he tell? They say the Lionheart is preparing to march on Jerusalem.'

'Now?' Judith said in astonishment. 'But they were in the middle of peace negotiations!'

'They are always talking about peace,' her hostess replied with a sigh. 'It does not stop them fighting. If the King should march on Jerusalem, the whole Saracen host will oppose him and much blood will be shed before the Holy City is lost or won.'

Judith's eyes grew wide and troubled. Despite Geoffrey's comment about the King and the Sultan 'playing' at peace talks she had not realised that a battle might flare up so suddenly. Geoffrey would, of course, fight beside the King. Many men would die. She recalled Hasan, saying that he would kill Geoffrey 'with exquisite pleasure' if they met on the field.

And she had let him walk out, without a word from her. But she had not realised that he might be riding to battle! She had thought he would return within a day or two.

Noting her distress, Xenia laid a comforting hand on her arm. 'Did he not tell you, child?'

'He told me nothing!' Judith cried. 'He thinks I am so stupid that I understand nothing. It's true that many things in Outremer are new to me and I—I have made mistakes. Is that any reason he should abandon me?'

'He has not abandoned you, my dear. But he has duties that call him away. A crusader knight is not his own master. And Geoffrey must love you, or he would not have married you. Why, the last time I saw him he was talking of taking holy vows and becoming a full brother of the order of St John.'

Judith's brow knotted. 'Was he?' she said faintly, unable to fathom the import of that news.

'Indeed he was. Marriage was the last thing on his mind, especially since he has no inheritance to hope for. You are an heiress, are you?'

'No,' Judith said miserably. 'I possess nothing.'

Smiling, Xenia patted her arm. 'It was love that brought you together, then. Like Demetrios and me. When did you meet Sir Geoffrey?'

'When I arrived in Acre.' Realising that she couldn't possibly tell the true story, she decided on half-truths. 'His father—my guardian Earl Torquil—arranged the match. I have a brother, named Edwin, who ran away to join the King. The Earl assumed he would not return, in which case I would inherit my father's lands, and so he betrothed me to Geoffrey. I came in search of my brother, and met Geoffrey—'

'And fell in love with him and married him,' Xenia finished for her, her deep-set eyes smoky with dreams of young romance.

Although it could not have been further from the truth, Judith nodded. What had happened in Megiddo now seemed like a nightmare, all caused by her own impulsiveness.

'What of your brother?' Xenia asked. 'Did you find him?'

Judith laid a hand to her head to hide her tears. 'Almost. He is with the garrison at Acre. Geoffrey promised to find him for me, but—' But Geoffrey had forgotten that promise, had he not? He had got rid of the 'thorn in his flesh' at the first possible moment and gone about his duties without a thought for her. Suppose some ill should befall Edwin, either in battle or from the diseases which decimated the Crusader armies in this hot land? Then she would inherit Claverham, and Earl Torquil's plan would be fulfilled. Had that been in the back of Geoffrey's mind?

Such bitter thoughts were her constant companions as the days passed. She grew more and more uncertain about the future, more worried about Edwin, but tried to conceal her restlessness from Xenia. The June days were hot and humid, the air full of dust, with flies buzzing everywhere.

Jaffa was a pleasant town, its white houses decked with laurels and vines, doors and windows protected from the sun by red cloth which shed a pleasant pink glow. The heavy scent of sheep and goats pervaded the air, mixed with odours of cooking oil, musk, sandalwood, and aromatic herbs which smouldered in braziers to keep disease away.

Since Xenia's husband was a wealthy man, their house was hung with Persian tapestries, while the floors were formed from brightly-coloured pieces of tile made into mosaic patterns. Dishes of copper gleamed in the cool rooms, and carved ivory boxes held preserved fruits, fragrant spices and almond paste. Judith lacked for nothing, yet how could she be content?

Sometimes she visited the bazaar with Xenia and on one visit she was tempted to dip into her small store of money to purchase some fine material to fashion a new gown. Other days they went down to the harbour to check on one of Demetrios' ships as it loaded or unloaded. Demetrios trusted his wife with the duties of overseer in his absence and Judith thought how very different Xenia's life was from her own, with useful things to do, a home to run, and a husband who loved and valued her.

Despite the peace of the town, however, its inhabitants could not forget that the land was at war. Almost daily, provision caravans set out to take supplies and water to the crusading army, which was now camped in the waterless hills several miles from Jerusalem, and more than once Judith saw the remnants of those caravans straggle back after being devastated by Saracen raiders.

Every time a messenger pounded through the streets to the citadel, she held her breath, fearing that the battle had begun. And at night she endured horrific dreams in which she saw Geoffrey slain, or Edwin lying covered in blood. During the day she consoled herself that Edwin, at least, was safe in Acre. What was certain was Geoffrey's peril, and in her dreams it was usually Hasan who cut him down before advancing on her purposefully.

Almost as bad were times when sleep would bring pictures of Geoffrey's return and she imagined herself running into his arms, only to wake and find him still absent and the possibility of a happy reunion as distant as the stars. Too much lay between them. She hated him and he despised her. A fine basis for a marriage! Driven half-frantic by waiting in the heat, she began to think that if only she could see Edwin then her worries would be less. If only she could get back to Acre!

A chance remark of Xenia's made her seize the chance it offered—one of Demetrios' ships, now loading in Jaffa harbour, would call in at Acre to pick up more goods on its way to Cyprus.

'Let me take passage on the ship,' she begged her hostess. 'Please, Xenia! This waiting for news near sends me mad. There is nothing I can do here, but in Acre I might occupy myself in finding Edwin. I can pay for my passage.'

'I can't let you go, child,' Xenia said. 'Sir Geoffrey left you in my keeping. He'd be angry if I let you go alone.'

'I came from Cyprus on my own,' Judith replied passionately. 'I shall die of despair if you keep me here! All I have to do is think and my thoughts are not comfortable companions. I fear for Geoffrey's safety, but there is nothing I can do. My brother I might find.

Xenia, he's nothing but a lad. Only fifteen. No—he will be sixteen by now, he was born in June. I *must* go on that ship. I beg you, Xenia!'

The merchant's wife looked troubled but her kindly nature could not withstand such pleading and she knew that her guest had been suffering mental torment since the day she arrived. She agreed, though reluctantly, and put Judith into the personal care of the ship's master, charging him with her safety until they reached Acre.

Once again Judith stood on the prow of a merchant ship, enjoying the sea wind in her face as the harbour of Acre came into sight, but this time she knew what she would do when she reached shore—she would go to the Queen and beg for help.

When finally she reached the castle, the steward recognised her and sent for Lady Elena to conduct her to the Queen's bower. She found Berengaria ill, lying on her bed looking pallid, but otherwise nothing had changed—the ladies were still bored, still waiting for the King's return.

Judith apologised for the way she had disappeared, but Queen Berengaria forgave her at once. It was the Lady Joan who snorted and demanded to know where Judith had been.

'I was trying to find my brother,' Judith said. 'We were attacked and I was separated from my escort. Then I met Sir Geoffrey de Belgarde and—'

'It was he you ran after!' Lady Joan said furiously. 'And have you been with him these six weeks? For shame, Judith of Claverham! You are no better than a common camp-follower. And where is he now, your handsome knight? Gone off and left you, so you come whining back to us.'

'My lady!' Judith began hotly, but was stilled by a gesture from the Queen's pale hand as Lady Joan turned and stamped away.

'She is not herself,' Berengaria breathed. 'She has been angry ever since she heard that my lord the King had offered her in marriage to the Sultan's brother.'

Judith sat down on a stool beside the Queen's bed, helping her to sip orange juice from a silver cup. 'It has not been as the Lady Joan says, I swear. Sir Geoffrey and I are married. He left me safe in Jaffa before returning to the King's side, and I have not seen him since that day. I came back to Acre to find my brother. My lady—will you help me? My brother is with the garrison here somewhere.'

'We shall enquire,' Berengaria said. 'But there is no hurry. We must await the return of the King. I shall ask him to find your brother for you. Ah, Judith, I am glad to see you again. You have such a gentle way, and such cool hands . . .'

She seemed too sick for Judith to press the matter of finding Edwin, though it was frustrating to be so near at last and still be prevented from seeing him.

Settling back into the enervating routine of the bower, Judith found it hard to contain her impatience. The ladies did their embroideries, or spun thread, or wove at the loom in that tower room with its views over the ocean, and they talked, and talked. The subject of Judith's marriage provided a topic for much gossip, with acid comment from Lady Joan. It was almost unheard of for a poor knight to marry a girl without a dowry and the ladies agreed that such a match could never prosper. Everything conspired to make Judith more depressed.

Eventually she went to see the captain of the guard, who promised to make enquiries about her brother, but when the answer came it brought her no comfort— Edwin of Claverham was not to be found among the garrison of Acre. But someone remembered the red-bearded giant who had been his constant companion. It was thought that Magnus, and his young master, had gone with the contingent which had marched to join the main army in the hills near Jerusalem.

Judith was relieved to know that Magnus had survived his struggle with the Bedouin, but the rest was bad news. If the King should march on Jerusalem then Edwin, as a footsoldier without proper armour, would be in even greater peril than Geoffrey. She wished that she had never left Jaffa.

Then word came that King Richard, after long deliberations and quarrels among his leading barons, had decided that a siege of Jerusalem would be too chancy in high summer. The Saracens had made sure that there was no drinkable water outside the city, and the Crusaders' provision caravans were under constant attack; they could not be sure of maintaining a supply of water during a lengthy siege, and so, in view of the heat and dust, the army was retreating to the coastal towns of Outremer. Richard had, however, sent a message to Saladin warning him not to regard the retreat as a victory. 'The ram backs for bucking,' was the way he worded it.

Judith stood on the ramparts of the citadel with Lady Joan, shading her eyes as the long columns of men came into sight—footsoldiers flanking the squadrons of mounted knights, with a baggage-train snaking alongside. At their head the King rode between fluttering banners. He was, Judith saw, astride a milk-white horse—the horse she had ridden from Megiddo. Was Geoffrey with him? And Edwin?

'So he comes, at last,' Lady Joan said grimly. 'I shall go and meet him. I have a word to say to that brother of mine.'

In the bower, Judith found the Queen risen from her sick-bed, being laced into a bright yellow gown by Matilda while Elena braided the lank, mouse-brown hair. Berengaria looked more nervous than delighted at the prospect of a reunion with her husband, and sweat stood on her parchment-pale brow.

They all went down to the great hall to greet the King, who strode in frowning, surrounded by a crowd of knights and barons. He was a handsome man with a mane of golden hair, tall and strong—the greatest knight in Christendom, before whom the armies of Saladin trembled. So the minstrels sang. But he seemed an indifferent husband, for after he had bowed over Berengaria's hand he appeared to forget her existence as he turned away to talk with his advisers.

Lady Joan came up, spots of angry colour burning on her face. 'You should not have left your bed, my lady,' she said to the Queen. 'The King is busy with affairs of state. He ignored me when I tried to speak to him. There are rumours that our brother John is making mischief in England, and Richard is anxious to be done with this war and go home to secure the kingdom.'

'Then we shall retire to the bower,' Berengaria said

softly, but Judith glimpsed tears in her eyes and felt sorry
for the young Queen. Her own hopes had been tempor-
arily deflated, too, for among the knights who crowded
into the hall there was no sign of Geoffrey de Belgarde.
Only Lady Elena was happy: her lord the Baron Hum-
frey had returned. Judith saw the pair embracing in a
quiet corner and thought dully that her own reunion with
her husband was not likely to be so tender.

That evening the Queen declared that she felt better
and would dine with the King at his banquet in the great
hall. All the ladies accompanied her and seemed
cheered by the company of the men, though Judith,
being the lowliest of their number, waited on the Queen
at table, standing behind her chair in the shadows
thrown by the torches.

At the high table the King wore his golden circlet and
a cloak of bright scarlet, flanked by his wife and his
sister, along with the most important lords of his court,
while at the long tables down the hall his more junior
lieutenants, the leading knights, laughed and drank
wine, flinging bones to the dogs. They were entertained
by an Arab juggler, a group of black tumblers, and by
the King's minstrel Blondel, who sang ballads telling of
the Lionheart's bold deeds in battle, particularly the
fight at Arsuf, when the Saracens had been soundly
defeated.

After the feast, as the company dispersed, Judith
approached one of the knights and asked him if he knew
where Sir Geoffrey de Belgarde might be found.

'I have not seen him since we broke camp before
Jerusalem four days ago,' the man replied, looking her
over boldly. 'But if it's company you seek—'

'Thank you, sir,' she said with a sigh, backing away. 'But it is not.'

She followed the other ladies to the bower, irritated by the overpowering feeling of loneliness which had suddenly assailed her. At least she knew that Geoffrey had been alive four days ago. He had probably gone to Jaffa. Or was he off making more overtures of peace? She had heard the King say that he intended to sail for England as soon as possible, but he could not desert the Holy cause without at least agreeing a truce with Saladin. Presumably Geoffrey would be involved as envoy again. How long would it be before he came?

She wept into her pillow that night, wishing she had stayed with Xenia instead of insisting on this fruitless trip to Acre. Edwin's whereabouts were uncertain, and Geoffrey . . . For all she knew, Geoffrey might even now be back in Megiddo, near Mariamne. If he had made time for a visit to Jaffa then she had missed seeing him. All her actions seemed to lead her astray.

Early the following morning, however, as she dressed and made ready for another day of endless waiting, a page appeared at the door of the bower asking for her. Judith's heart leapt and began to hammer as she looked at the freckle-faced lad.

'You have a message for me?'

'Yes, my lady. Sir Geoffrey de Belgarde asks that you attend him in the courtyard. He said he'd wait by the postern gate. You are to come at once.'

Such a message—a summons, in effect—was typical of him! But despite her annoyance her feet flew down the circling stairs.

The courtyard hummed with activity: servants rushing

about on chores and errands, soldiers and horses, chickens, dogs . . . The return of the King had filled the castle to overflowing and it appeared that many of his men had bedded down in the courtyard the previous night.

As she edged through the throng, Judith's step slowed, her doubts increased and she remembered that her relationship with Geoffrey was far from happy. He had married her because he had had no choice; he regarded her as a nuisance. What would he say to her now?

She saw him beyond a straggling group of soldiers on their way to seek breakfast, and the sight of him made her spirits droop even lower, for he had no smile to greet her. Instead a frown drew his brows into furrows and his mouth looked hard, his lips pressed together. As she approached him she saw his eyes—those beautiful eyes of gold-flecked green with their fringe of thick lashes— they were underlined with weary shadows and their expression chided her, with no hint of pleasure at the sight of her.

Fearing that he might see her disappointment, she lowered her own eyes, staring at the white cross on his tunic.

'You may well look ashamed,' he muttered. 'I told you to stay with Xenia. What if some harm had befallen you?'

'Then your problems would have ended,' she said dully.

'Aye, it's true you seem to bring me only trouble,' he agreed. 'I went straight to Jaffa and found you gone. Which was a pity, because I took your brother with me—and that red-headed serf of his.'

She lifted her head, her face lighting. 'Edwin? You found him?'

Even the sight of her hope-filled eyes seemed not to move him, except that he lifted one corner of his mouth in a wry, humourless smile. 'As I promised I would. I do not forget promises.'

'Finding Edwin brings you nearer to being rid of me,' she replied in an undertone. 'Is my brother well?'

It was as though a cloud crossed his eyes—a cloud that made her catch her breath in alarm, her eyes dilating.

'Wait!' Geoffrey grasped her shoulders, giving her a little shake. 'It is a fever, nothing more. Many of us suffered from it in the desert heat. I left him in Xenia's care and came straight to fetch you. Two days' hard riding, my lady. It will take us two more days, at least, to go back.'

Staring at him, Judith saw that the dark lines under his eyes were not mere weariness. 'Have you been ill, too?'

'A little, but I am recovered now. Do not concern yourself. We must return to Jaffa with all speed, for the King will send for me soon and I must be ready.'

'Could we—' she ventured. 'Could we find a ship? It is so much easier to travel by sea.'

'Aye, and more costly. You seem to forget that I have no money.'

'But I have. Arrange passage for us on any ship you can find, and pay what you must.'

As she offered him her purse, he hesitated, as if he might refuse the offer, but at last he took the money and said, 'Make ready. I shall send word when it is arranged.'

She watched his tall figure as he strode with lithe grace among the crowd in the courtyard, and her eyes misted with stupid tears. He was in a hurry to be gone, it seemed. Once he had her in Jaffa, with Edwin, he would no doubt make equal haste to arrange for another, longer passage for her—back to England.

The ship was a dhow, fat-bellied but graceful, its deck piled with boxes of glass and pottery from Antioch and purple samite made by the weavers of Acre. Near the bow a tent had been stretched to provide a little privacy for the two passengers during the coming night—Geoffrey had been generous with the passage money.

'But you still have the opal pendant,' he reminded Judith. 'That, and the money you have left, will buy you passage to England for yourself and your brother, though the serf may have to make shift as a sailor.'

'Then we shall be out of your way,' she said carelessly. 'Tomorrow when we reach Jaffa your responsibilities for me will end.'

He was leaning on the side of the ship, the wind lifting his hair as the sailors raised the sail to catch the breeze, but he turned his head to give her a long, considering look. 'Aye, I know,' he said quietly.

'And you will be relieved for that.'

'It may be so.'

'May be? You have told me often enough—' She stopped, aware that he was watching her mouth, making the nerves in her lips prickle.

'But first there is one more night,' he said under his breath.

Judith turned away, staring up at the tower which stood as defence to the entrance of Acre harbour, while the ship moved out towards the open sea. She stole a sidelong look at the tent which was intended for their sleeping quarters, wondering if Geoffrey would dare attempt to make love to her there, within hearing of the crew of the dhow. Did he calculate that she would be forced to lie quiet, or risk the ribaldry of the Arab sailors?

Sailing with the brisk westerly wind, the ship plied southward, always within sight of the land, until evening shadows hid the arid coastline and the night brought the stars to shine. Geoffrey spent most of the time talking with the ship's master, and to judge from their gestures the sailor was telling him about the stars. Eventually, however, he made his way across the heaving deck to where Judith stood clinging to the side.

'Are you tired?' he asked, peering at her by the light of a flickering torch fastened by the mast.

'No, not at all,' she lied. 'Besides, I could not sleep with the ship tossing like this.'

'There does seem to be a heavy swell. But the master tells me he expects squalls before the night is out. Perhaps you should rest while you can.'

'I am comfortable here.'

He reached a hand to her chin, making her look at him, and she saw the mocking gleam in his eyes. The uncertain torchlight, spitting and fluttering in the wind, made his face look darker than ever, like that of a demon with brilliant eyes that saw through to her soul.

'You need have no fear,' he said softly. 'I shall not trouble you. If this marriage goes unconsummated, you may seek an annulment. I shall not put difficulties in your way.'

Dismay made a stillness inside her. 'Annulment?'

'That would seem to be the best answer for us both. The only witnesses to the ceremony were Muslim—and Muslims do not count under Christian law.'

She jerked away from him, staring into the sea-darkness with tears stinging her eyes. Of course that would be the way he planned it—to be free of all commitment to her. Not that she could blame him, deep in her heart. She had no prospect of a dowry now that Edwin was safe. All she had accomplished by her futile journey to Outremer had been to return the situation to the way it had been before Edwin ran from Castle Belgarde. Until he came of age, five long years from now, he would remain in the power of Earl Torquil, and his safety might still be in jeopardy. All Judith's trials had changed nothing.

A sad smile curved her lips as she thought ruefully that one thing had changed, after all: she would have to live now with an ache in her heart. Because of Earl Torquil's son! The irony made her bite her lip against a sob of painful laughter.

'You shall go to your Priory undefiled,' Geoffrey said softly. 'Though it grieves me to allow it.'

'It would grieve you to leave any woman undefiled!' she snapped.

His hand on her shoulder whirled her round to see him frowning with fury. 'My lady, have a care. My honour is all I have. Insult that and you insult my existence.'

'Then prove yourself honourable!' she retorted in a fierce whisper, shrugging free of his grasp. 'Do not touch me again!'

'Is it dishonourable for a man to touch his wife?' he asked with a wry little smile that appeared to have sadness in it—though Judith told herself the flaring torchlight was playing tricks on her eyes. 'Very well.' He moved a little away from her and leaned on the ship's side, his head tipped back to stare at the stars. 'Did you know that sailors find their way at night by the stars? The Arabs have made it into an art.'

'Indeed?' she replied, her eyes on a dark mass in the sky that was rapidly swallowing the starlight. 'And what do they use when clouds cover the stars?'

Before he could reply, a violent gust of wind swept the ship, heaving it to one side. Judith, taken off guard, found herself thrown by the elements into Geoffrey's arms. He held her tightly, bracing himself against the vessel's sudden lurching, yelling at her to hold on to the side.

The wind grew fiercer. Judith heard the snap of a breaking rope as the cargo shifted. Boxes fell across the deck, wood and pottery shattering. The ship heeled drunkenly on its side, veering suddenly off course. Shouts and roared orders filled the night as the torches blinked out one by one, unable to withstand the rising wind. In the tumult, Judith clung desperately to the gunwale, held there by her husband's strength as he sheltered her with his body, his hands braced either side of her.

The master's voice sounded from close at hand, shouting something at Geoffrey, who replied in kind. Then the ship juddered. Judith gasped as she was crushed to the side by Geoffrey's weight. She heard rocks scrape as the ship swung round dizzyingly and the sail tore from its ropes to stream against the black sky like a spectre.

Another shudder ran through the ship. Judith felt

Geoffrey torn from his protective stance and as she screamed his name the ship reared like a maddened horse. Her hands lost their grip. She was tossed helplessly into foaming waves. The sea closed over her, the tide rolling her like driftwood. Spluttering and gasping, she gulped at fresh air, and felt the water tear at her clothes as she was dragged again beneath the black sea.

CHAPTER
SEVEN

MIRACULOUSLY, just as drowning seemed certain, firm sand bumped against her tumbling body. Wet and shifting, it stirred as the waves surged up onto the shore. Another breaker doused her, choking her, flinging her further onto the sand, and when it retreated she found herself kneeling on the very edge of the ocean. She forced herself to her feet, staggered a few steps, and collapsed on soft, dry sand, gasping for breath.

'Judith!' Geoffrey's yell came out of the scream of the wind. 'Judith!'

At that moment the cloud whipped away from the moon as if someone had drawn a curtain, showing her the tall figure that raced down the beach towards her. He threw himself down beside her just as a terrible screech came from the stricken ship. It was jammed onto the shore, partly on black rocks, partly on the sand, keeled over at an angle with its cargo tumbled into the sea. But as Judith looked at it she saw something else—a band of horsemen riding out of the sand-dunes with lifted swords, yelling a war-cry as they rode into the waves slashing right and left at the helpless sailors.

'They're after booty,' Geoffrey said hoarsely, grasping her arm. 'Quickly, my lady. We must hide while they are too busy to see us.'

Hampered by her wet skirts, she scrambled to her feet, hearing a scream of terror that stopped short in a horrific gurgle. Geoffrey's hand on her arm urged her on, among the deep shadows thrown by the heaped sand of the dunes, until the cries of the massacre grew faint in the distance and he allowed her to rest.

She lay on her side in the sand, recovering her breath and beginning to shiver as the night wind struck cold through her soaked clothes. Beside her, Geoffrey lay listening, his head cocked to catch any sound that came above the wind. Eventually, faintly, Judith heard the drumming of hooves as the marauding band galloped away—in the opposite direction.

'Thank God,' Geoffrey said fervently. 'I have nothing with which to defend you. I lost my sword in the sea.'

'We almost lost our lives,' she replied, her voice little more than a croak, but her hand sought the purse at her waist and found it still secure. She had, however, lost her veil and her bronze circlet.

'Without my sword we may as well be dead if those Bedouin find us,' he told her. 'Wait here, my lady, and keep watch.'

'Where are you going?' she gasped, but he was already striding for the beach.

Judith got to her feet, brushing at the sand that caked her. She was in a hollow among the dunes and the brisk wind from the sea sent little eddies of sand whirling in misty moonlight. Struggling against her wet, clogged gown, she threw off her dripping mantle and draped it across her arm as she set out in the direction Geoffrey had gone. Soon she came to the beach, where some distance away the shape of the wrecked ship was visible, with white foam breaking round it. Though she strained her eyes and ears, she could detect no sign of danger.

After a while Geoffrey's dark figure appeared, loping across the sand. He showed her the leather water-bottle and the long knife he had slung on a strap round his shoulder. Possession of the weapon seemed to make him feel more secure and Judith forbore to ask where he had found it since she was sure it must have come from the body of one of the sailors. She was shivering uncontrollably, from the cold and from apprehension.

'Are they all dead?' she managed.

'Aye,' he said grimly. 'We must move on. That will keep us warm.'

'Move in the darkness? But—do you know where we are?'

'No—and that is why we cannot stay here. This water will not last long—the bottle is scarce half-full. God knows how far we must walk to find fresh water and the sunrise will come too soon. We must move along the beach, southward towards Jaffa.'

Knowing he was probably right, she trudged beside him, though very soon her feet became sore. She had left off her stockings in the summer heat and the sand that clung to her shoes acted as an abrasive. Gasping at Geoffrey to stop, she tore off the shoes and stretched her aching feet, sensing his irritation at being hampered by her yet again, though he said nothing.

With her shoes in one hand and the other holding her skirts clear of the ground, she forced her legs on. To their left the sand-dunes were backed by dark hills, while to the right the sea sighed and rippled. Water dripped from her thick braided hair to soak her gown further, but that discomfort was as nothing beside the torment in her ill-used limbs.

When she looked up, she saw with dismay that ahead loomed an outcrop of cliffs, with the sea washing at their feet.

'We must go inland,' Geoffrey said, nodding to where the low dunes ran into a rise of ground that was an outlier of the cliffs.

'I must rest first,' she sighed, sinking down at the edge of the dunes with limbs that felt stiff and sore.

'Very well.' He sounded reluctant. 'But not for long.' He relieved her of her damp mantle and spread it to dry, laying his own cloak beside it and anchoring both with stones before he, too, sat down not far from her.

He was not made of iron, Judith thought, watching him from her eye-corner. His slumped shoulders and bent head reminded her that he had only lately recovered from illness himself, and when she remembered how nearly she had lost him to the sea her hands ached to touch him and offer comfort.

'It will be easier travelling by daylight,' she said.

'It will be hotter, too,' he replied. 'We must press on.'

'But we cannot be so far from water! There are streams, and oases. We shall find them better when the sun rises.'

'No. We must go on.'

With a heavy sigh, she lay back against the slope of the dune, realising that the wind had dropped a little and the air seemed less chill. Geoffrey leaned over her, supported on one arm as he looked down at her shadowed face.

'Sleep if you wish,' he said. 'Just for an hour. I will keep watch.'

'You are tired, too,' she objected.

'Aye, but it is nothing new to me. I am strong.'

'Usually you are. How long have you been recovered from the fever?'

'Long enough,' he replied, and when she would have argued he laid his fingers across her lips, startling her into silence. 'Lady, do not concern yourself for me.'

'A woman should concern herself over her husband's health,' she said sombrely.

'But I shall not be your husband for much longer,' he reminded her. His fingers stroked her cheek as if, having touched her, he was unable to withdraw from contact. Gently he pushed stray strands of hair from her brow, looping them behind her ear, continuing down the line of her chin to touch her lips again with a hand that trembled.

Very slowly, he bent over her, kissing her softly in a way that sent tremors through her. Unable to deny what she felt, she let her hands creep behind his neck, her fingers sliding into his hair. With a groan he lay down beside her, his mouth hardening into urgency, warming her with its heat.

When he lifted his head, she stared breathlessly into his face, wondering if she imagined the tenderness in him. She was unable to see him clearly in the uncertain moonlight, but she fancied there was no mockery in his eyes.

'I thought you had drowned,' she whispered.

'And I you,' he replied, kissing her with growing

fever, one arm behind her head to hold her close to him. His free hand fumbled with the strings that tied her chemise at the neck and she felt his fingers against her skin. Then he touched the chain of the pendant and became still, drawing back as he brought the opal from between her breasts and stared at it.

'You are fortunate to have a rich admirer,' he said gruffly. 'I could not give you jewels.'

'It is for—for my passage home,' she muttered.

'Aye, so it is.' She saw his mouth twist as he laid the heavy gem back in place and let his fingers trail over the curves beneath her gown, his gaze following the movement. Then abruptly he wrenched away from her and sat with his arms clasped tightly about his knees, staring at the whispering sea.

'I never desired jewels,' she said softly. 'Besides, Hasan gave it to me to annoy you. You said so. He means nothing to me.'

Glancing round, he gave her a bitter smile. 'You think me jealous of him? Nay, lady, you mistake me. The jewel reminded me of Megiddo and my duty to the King. The Lionheart is in earnest to seek peace now, since he is anxious to go home. He will need my services.'

She scrambled to her knees, clutching the opal, filled with a heady fury which she knew was jealousy. 'Will you return to Megiddo?'

'I shall go wherever my duties take me.'

'In the hopes of seeing the Princess Mariamne?' she demanded.

In the moonlight, she saw his eyes flash anger. 'I shall go to see the Sultan! My business is with him, not his niece.'

'No? Will you deny that you are in love with her, and she with you?'

'I do deny it!'

She did not believe him. She had seen Mariamne, had witnessed the way Geoffrey spoke to her that night after the Turkish girl had tried to kill her. Of course he was in love with her. Her jealous heart could find no other explanation.

'Xenia told me you had spoken of taking holy vows,' she informed him. 'Is that true?'

'I have considered it, yes.'

'Because you cannot have Mariamne!' she cried. 'You would turn monk because of unrequited passion!'

In a whirl of motion he turned on her, grabbing her wrists as she tried to fend him off, forcing her backwards so that she fell onto the sand, her arms imprisoned above her head while he heaved himself to lie on top of her, his weight preventing her from moving. 'My passion shall not remain unrequited,' he growled into her face. 'You are my wife, mistress Judith. Will you pay your wifely dues now?'

'Never!'

He bent to kiss her and when she turned her head away he took both her wrists in one hand and used the other to force her lips back to his. Helpless, she squirmed beneath him, hating the scrape of his teeth and the roughness of stubble on his chin, but all at once his mouth became tender, making sweet pain flood through all her veins. She was aware of his need for her, and now her own need rose to meet it, though she hated him for having such power over her senses.

'Is it still "never"?' he demanded hoarsely.

'And always shall be!' she said in a ragged whisper. 'You are beyond contempt. Wanting another woman, you would still make use of me, though you say you seek an annulment to this hateful marriage. You remind me more of your father with every day that passes. He uses people, too—uses them, and then discards them at his pleasure.'

Cursing under his breath, he rolled away from her and leapt to his feet, his breathing sounding husky in the suddenly-quiet night. The wind had dropped and only the sighing of the sea murmured in the darkness. Over-head the stars stood bright against a sky like black velvet, and the moon hung low over the landward hills.

'I forgot you bore my father such hatred,' he said through his teeth.

'Hatred he has well earned!' Judith choked, trying to hide the tears that threatened to engulf her.

'He did his duty under the law,' he argued. 'Since your father died—'

'Or since he was murdered!' She had hoped never to make the accusation, but such was her distress that the words were torn out of her. She heard Geoffrey catch his breath. Unable to look at him, she began to unbraid her hair, to let it dry more easily.

'My lady,' Geoffrey said in a low, warning voice, 'have you any proof to give credence to such an allegation?'

'None,' she admitted. 'Except that the Earl had long hated my father and sworn vengeance on him. Then one day he invited my father to go hunting, and when they returned my father was dead—because a horse which he rode every day, which was as docile as a fawn, had suddenly bolted and thrown him. We found a wound on the horse's flank, as if it had been cut with a whip, but it was not proof. And so the Earl laid claim to the Claverham lands and put me in the Priory.'

'As was his right!'

She lifted her head defiantly. 'So it was, sir. And by right of law he took Edwin into his household.'

'To train him as a knight!' he exclaimed impatiently. 'My father is not an easy man. I admit it. But a great lord must sometimes appear harsh. I do not believe he would stoop to murder.'

Judith climbed to her feet, her hair flowing about her like a silver mantle beneath the moon. 'You are his son. I do not expect you to believe me. But he prevented me from communicating with my brother. And he abused Edwin. Magnus told me so. Do you wonder that my brother ran away? And now—' she spread her hands helplessly, palms-upward, staring at their pale slenderness. 'Now all will be as it was before. We remain in the Earl's power.'

'Perhaps not,' Geoffrey said quietly.

'Is there another way?' she asked, but what she saw in his face frightened her. 'Geoffrey, what—'

'I thought it best not to tell you—not to worry you,' he said with a frown. 'But your brother is more sick than I told you. He may not live to inherit his lands.'

Trembling as if with ague, she stared at him uncomprehendingly.

'In which case you will be an heiress,' he added. 'You will be able to take a husband.'

'But *you* are my—' She stopped, her brain racing.

'If you suspect me of being party to my father's plots then you misjudge me, lady,' he said tightly.

'Why did you not tell me Edwin was so sick?' she cried.

'I told you why—there seemed no point in alarming you. But perhaps now you better understand my hurry to reach Jaffa. Put your shoes ón. We had best be moving before the moon sets.'

Alarm lent her muscles more strength for a while as they climbed into the arid hills, but it was not long before the moon went down and with only starlight to guide them their progress was slow. Eventually Geoffrey decided it might be wiser to rest until dawn, though this time he hardly spoke to her as he watched her curl up to sleep. He himself sat with his back against a rock, the long sailor's knife ready in one hand.

Despite the doubts and fears in her mind, Judith's young body demanded respite and sleep soon came to soothe her fevered thoughts.

When she woke, the sun was already lifting above the hills, though Geoffrey had said they must move at dawn. She saw that he had fallen asleep at his post, his dark head bent over his knees, but his hand still clasped the hilt of the knife whose sharp blade glinted in the sunlight. As she stood up, a stick cracked under her foot and Geoffrey came awake, and alert, instantly, reminding her of his Turkish name—Mountain Lion. He did seem to possess the instincts of a wild animal.

His tunic bore traces of salt deposits and her own clothes were in a similar state, her hair a thick tangle. His gaze made her even more aware of her unkempt condition, though his own was scarcely better: tousled dark hair fell half over those disturbing green-gold eyes, and a growth of stubble showed against his tan.

'You should have woken me before,' he said, handing her the water-bottle.

'I was sleeping until a moment ago,' she replied, and tilted the bottle to her parched lips, taking just enough to wet her throat. She watched as he followed suit before shaking the bottle, frowning over the little it contained.

'Come,' he said, replacing the knife in its sheath. 'We must be on our way.'

Before them lay nothing but hostile hills, the soil dry with summer, supporting only a few blades of grass and the ubiquitous cedar scrub that showed in odd patches of green against the general dust-yellow. In places there were rocks to be negotiated, where Geoffrey offered his hand to help her, though his touch seemed impersonal now.

After a while they came to a broad valley, as arid as the rest of the countryside, with little dust-devils swirling in the wind that was slowly rising. The sun lifted ever higher, its heat searing the land. Judith wrapped her mantle about her head to shade her face as she trudged on, bent into the wind, but she knew she could not go much further before she collapsed from the heat and exhaustion.

They had one more drink each, after which the bottle was empty. Geoffrey hung it back on its strap round his shoulder, saying that he would fill it when they found more water; then he took Judith's hand, studying her face with a frown.

'We must keep going,' he said firmly.

Each step became torture. Her feet dragged and her mouth was dry. She would have stopped several times but he tugged at her hand and forced her on. She began to hate him for his relentless bullying, though she knew that he acted for the best.

Hot dust, thrown up by the wind, engulfed them suddenly, scouring Judith's skin, half-blinding her even through her mantle. Geoffrey used his cloak as a shield, trying to protect her from the worst of the choking storm by bending over her with his arm lifted, his other hand still round hers to make her keep walking.

To her relief, the dust soon cleared, its cloud racing on across the valley. Her shaking legs buckled. Half-fainting, she flopped to the ground, and at the same moment she heard the beating of hooves. Lifting aching eyes, she saw a horseman storming towards them through the retreating dust-cloud—a Saracen, by his clothing, for he wore a turban with bands of material drawn round his face, and his robes swept behind him in the wind.

Swiftly, Geoffrey drew his knife and stood in front of Judith, braced against the earth as if to meet the charge of the enemy. But a few yards away the horseman drew rein, making his mount dance, and leapt from the saddle throwing off the disguising veils. Judith's heart jerked with both relief and alarm as she saw that it was Hasan.

'Put up your knife, el-Asad,' he said with a smile, and reached to take a water-bottle from his saddle-tree, brushing past Geoffrey to kneel beside Judith and offer her a drink. She took it gratefully, lifting the bottle to her lips to let the cool, life-giving liquid trickle down her throat. She drank more, and more, until Hasan took the bottle from her and handed it to Geoffrey.

'You treat your lady ill,' he said softly.

'Our ship was wrecked!' Geoffrey exclaimed.

Ignoring him, Hasan smiled at Judith. 'I have been watching you from the hills—I, and my men. We had word of a shipwreck, and when I saw you I knew it was my sweet Lady of the Moon. So I brought you water. I see you still wear my gift.'

Her hand went to the opal as if to hide it and she glimpsed Geoffrey's angry expression as he wiped the back of his hand across his mouth. Yet why should he be angry when Hasan had come to help? He had sworn he was not jealous of the handsome emir.

'You have endured much,' Hasan said with sympathy. 'You must be weary, Lady of the Moon. There is an oasis not two miles away, if you will allow me to escort you.'

Behind him, Geoffrey demanded, 'What were you doing in these hills, my lord?'

'Bringing heart to my men.' Hasan sprang lightly to his feet, poised like a dancer with hands on hips as his smile widened in the face of Geoffrey's scowl. 'My men, who are keeping watch over Outremer, as your Templars watch our lands. You know, el-Asad, that a truce has not yet been agreed, though I hear your King Richard is at last ready to talk seriously. He knows Jerusalem is beyond his grasp. And his brother is being troublesome back in England, is he not?'

'Your spies have long ears,' Geoffrey growled.

Laughing, Hasan moved a little away, drew his sword and waved it above his head as a signal to the watchers in the hills. Geoffrey's hand went to his knife but, seeing it, Hasan shook his head, his eyes sparkling. 'I told my men I might send for horses. The Lady of the Moon cannot walk much further, and since you appear incapable of taking proper care of her—'

Swearing softly, Geoffrey whipped the knife out. Judith gasped in alarm as Hasan's sword came to answer the challenge and the two of them stood eyeing each other guardedly.

'Geoffrey, no!' She leapt up and caught his arm, pleading with him. 'Do not let him anger you. He came to help us.'

'If he continues to question my competence I shall kill him!' he vowed passionately. 'She is my wife, Hasan. Would you allow me to behave with your wife as you behave with mine?'

The sword wavered. 'I would disembowel you first,' Hasan replied, and sheathed his weapon. 'Forgive me, my friend. I meant no insult. It amuses me to jest with you. And she *is* fair.'

Geoffrey looked down at Judith's anxious face, his gaze flickering hungrily over her. 'I know,' he said under his breath as he laid an arm about her, holding her close to his side as if to demonstrate his possession of her.

She allowed her head to rest lightly on his shoulder, saddened by that look in his eyes. He could be possessive now, but only because Hasan had wounded his pride. As soon as they reached Jaffa he would be off about his duties and probably bother no more with her—as long as Edwin was alive. Edwin must live! She must go to him swiftly.

Another rider emerged from a cleft in the hills, throwing a small dust-cloud behind him as he rode towards the trio. He brought two spare horses and Judith allowed herself to be helped up into the saddle, glad to have the weight off her aching feet. Geoffrey hauled himself onto the second mount and they set off with Hasan in the lead, making for the water-hole.

Date-palms clustered around the pool, and Bedouin tents flapped in the wind. Nearby, a lad sat playing music on a pipe as he watched over a herd of sheep, while his elders came out to stare at the newcomers, the women all muffled in veils. A few words from Hasan stilled their suspicions, however, and soon Judith was plunging her face into the pool to cool her fevered skin.

The Holy Land was a strange place, she thought, where enemies offered each other chivalry in between fierce-fought battles; and where nomadic natives like the Bedouin did not take sides but could turn from their peaceful flocks to play brigand when it suited them, robbing both Crusaders and Saracens.

The Bedouin women brought fruit to offer to the travellers and Judith sat beneath the shade of a palm tree biting into a fig whose juice tasted sharp and refreshing, while the men sat nearby talking.

'And so, el-Asad,' Hasan was saying, 'this time it is to be a real peace. What shall you do when the war is ended? Will you return to England, or stay in our warm and beautiful land?'

'I shall stay here in Outremer.'

Hasan sent a smiling look at Judith. 'You must visit me at Megiddo—as my honoured guest this time. My wives will be delighted to meet you. Already they dye their hair with henna, to resemble Frankish women— but such is their foolishness. You may persuade them otherwise. But my sister will not be there, I fear. The Sultan has found a suitable man to be her husband.'

Although his gaze did not even flicker towards Geoffrey, she felt sure that his words were directed at her husband. She glanced at him to see what effect the news had and met his eyes, seeing the mockery there. He knew what she was thinking and derided her for it.

'I should enjoy meeting your—your wives,' she told Hasan, having trouble over the plural. How many wives did he have? Not that she was ever likely to find out since she was going back to England very soon.

'It would be a delight for me, too,' he said, those bold black eyes gleaming.

Impatiently, Geoffrey got to his feet. 'If we are to reach Jaffa before sunset we must be on our way. I shall see that the horses are returned to you, lord Hasan.'

'Yes, we shall meet again,' Hasan replied, also coming to his feet to exchange a meaningful stare with the tall knight. 'I trust it will be at the council table and not on the field, el-Asad. Your King has proved to be a man of changeable moods. But perhaps this time he will prove sincere. Farewell. And you, al-Khatun.'

He bowed low before her, touching his breast, lips and forehead in salute before he turned on his heel and strode to where his horse was tethered. Muttering to himself, Geoffrey bent and jerked Judith to her feet, a hand clamped round her arm as he led her to the horses. Her legs felt stiff, but the water and fruit had revived her and she was anxious now to be with Edwin.

They rode on, each with a full water-bottle and a supply of fruit, not pushing the horses too hard in the full heat of the day. Judith kept her mantle over her head, for her face was already burning from the sun's glare.

'I hope there will be peace,' she remarked to fill the silence. 'Surely God does not want us to fight with the

Saracens. They revere our holy places as we do, and they seem a gentle, courteous people.'

'They are—except on the field of battle. You have not seen that side of them, my lady. You have seen only Hasan, who enjoys flirting with you only to annoy me.'

Piqued, she replied, 'I do not believe he does it to annoy you.'

'No, clearly not,' he said with disgust. 'Or you would not encourage him so openly.'

'I was being friendly!' she exclaimed. 'There is no harm—'

'Between a man and a woman such things are easily misinterpreted. It was not your place to say you would enjoy visiting him.'

'I only said I would like to meet his wives!'

'His wives would be appalled by your behaviour,' he told her roughly. 'Saracen women know their place.'

'But I am not Saracen,' she argued. 'We should have been in difficult straits—perhaps dead—if Hasan had not offered his help. He is a true gentleman. If that is the way of Muslims, then I respect them for their beliefs.'

He flung her a green-lightning glance, his face taut with fury, flushed with angry blood. 'Maybe I should turn Muslim instead of monk!'

'Sir!' She was genuinely shocked.

'Why not?' Geoffrey raged. 'You so admire them— and at least they have the freedom to take more than one wife. If one proves a termagant there is an alternative— and a feast of delights among a man's concubines.'

'Yes, that would suit you, with your hot blood,' she retorted bitterly. 'And who would you take for a second wife? Mariamne?'

'Aye. If I were a Muslim she would have me.'

Well aware that this was true, she winced inwardly, glad of the mantle that veiled her face. 'Is that why you would do it—for her sake? Best hurry, sir. She has been found a husband, and though Muslim men have their pick of ladies their women are in the same sorry state as Christians—forced to a choice of one all their days.'

'Well, you, at least, may have a second chance,' he reminded her, bringing her back to reality with a cold shock. He intended to seek an annulment, did he not? He would stay in Outremer while she returned to England—with Edwin, please God.

The landscape shimmered through her sudden tears, which she told herself were caused by fear for her brother. But as the horse moved beneath her she was only aware that it carried her ever nearer to Jaffa—to a final separation from this man who tormented her—this man whom she hated and loved with equal intensity.

CHAPTER
EIGHT

WHEN at last they reached Xenia's house, Judith threw herself from the saddle and hurried across the small courtyard, seeing the plump merchant's wife appear at the door, a smile creasing her face. Xenia hugged her warmly, saying how glad she was to see her safe.

'And my brother?' Judith asked.

'Past the crisis,' the Greek woman assured her. 'Still weak, but he will live. He has been anxious to see you. Come in, my dear. And you, Sir Geoffrey.'

In the main room, shaded from the sun by striped awnings across the window, Edwin lay on the couch. Judith paused in the doorway, trying to conceal her anxiety. Her brother looked desperately ill, with blue shadows in the hollows round his eyes. And he was thin, his pale hair grown lank and unkempt, but he managed a smile as she crossed the room and sank down on the floor beside him, reaching for his hand.

'Edwin!'

'Sister,' he replied, low-voiced, the warmth dying from his eyes as he glanced behind her to where Geoffrey stood.

She saw that her brother's face had lost its youthful roundness and despite his weakness it was apparent that his body had changed to young manhood since she last saw him. Worriedly, she stroked the damp hair from his brow.

'I have been looking for you ever since I came to Outremer,' she said. 'Why did you run away, Edwin?'

'You know why.' He slanted another bleak look at Geoffrey. 'There was no need for you to come after me, sister.'

'I thought there was. But enough of that. Now you must concentrate on getting well. And then we shall go home together.'

Stubborn lines hardened about his mouth and his blue eyes grew dark. 'No, Judith. You may go home if you choose, but not with me. I shall not go back to Castle Belgarde until I am of age to claim my inheritance.'

Taken aback, Judith glanced behind her to where Geoffrey was a silent spectator and met his tight-lipped glance. He had known that Edwin would prove difficult, it seemed, but he refused to help her.

'What else can you do?' she asked her brother.

'I shall find a place somewhere. I shall train for knighthood, and when I am skilled in arms, and of age, I shall go back and challenge Earl Torquil with the murder of my father!' Sweat broke out to bead his upper lip and he sank back against the cushions with a groan.

'Hush now,' Judith murmured, a hand to his damp forehead. 'You must not think of such things.'

'I think of nothing else!' Edwin said petulantly. 'Your journey was wasted, sister. Do you take me for a fool? You have betrayed me!'

She sat back as if he had slapped her. 'I?'

'Yes, you! The Earl hates us, yet you married his son. Geoffrey de Belgarde is no friend of mine. What plots have you hatched between you? Did you plan to have me tossed overboard some stormy night on our voyage home, so that you may have Claverham—you and your husband?'

'Edwin, no!' she cried. 'You cannot believe—'

'I do believe it! You are in league against me. That is why the Earl sent you here. Why else should he agree to this marriage, without a dowry? Why, Judith?'

Before she could form a reply, Xenia came padding in, greatly alarmed by Edwin's distress. She pushed Judith aside and bent to calm the youth, who had fallen into a fit of weeping.

Feeling numb, Judith got to her feet and backed away. This was not at all what she had expected. Edwin was no longer the malleable little brother she had once known. What would she do now? She turned to Geoffrey, not really expecting help from him, but the black fury she saw in his eyes appalled her.

'You both speak slander of a man who is too far away to defend himself,' he said in a charged undertone. 'But at least on one count you may ease your brother's mind—you and I shall not be married any longer than we must, Lady Judith. I shall make sure of that.'

He swung round and strode out, going back to his duties as if relieved to be rid of her company. Judith stared after him, filled with a nameless misery, and when she looked back at the couch she met Xenia's sympathetic expression.

'He is angry,' the merchant's wife said. 'He will forget this, never fear.'

But Geoffrey would not forget, she knew, and neither would she. His family and her family were sworn enemies and there could never be anything but bitterness and mistrust between them.

She took over the nursing of her brother and slowly a remnant of the bond between them was reforged, though Edwin would not talk of going home; if she raised the subject it only angered him and, sooner than risk another rift, Judith desisted. Neither did she mention her husband, though he was often in her thoughts, his memory bringing her nothing but anguish.

Magnus had also been accepted into Xenia's household and helped the man Zebulon with his chores. As Edwin grew stronger, the huge red-headed serf would carry him out into the courtyard to sit beneath the red awning, and bring him succulent tit-bits, while the maids flitted about on sandalled feet inside the cool house as the hot July days drifted by.

On an evening towards the end of the month, as the aroma of cooking lifted from the fire-pits in the courtyard, Judith climbed to the balcony to enjoy the cool breeze which always sprang up at that time of day. She watched the shadows lengthen across the harbour, thrown by the great walled citadel whose ramparts fell sheer to the sea, but a stirring in the town drew her attention. Trumpets blared from the walls and people ran shouting through the streets. The church bells began to ring, sounding the tocsin of alarm, and amid the furore a horseman came full-gallop down the steep lane. Even before he threw himself from the saddle at Xenia's gate, Judith had recognised him and started down the steps, her heart thudding with both joy and fear.

'Geoffrey!' She paused a few feet from him, stricken by the agitated look on his face. 'What is it?'

'The Saracens are at the gates,' he said breathlessly. 'Where is Xenia? You must take ship before the town falls.'

'But why have they attacked? There was to be a peace settlement.'

'Aye, so there was. But the King planned to attack Beirut before leaving for home, and the Sultan's spies got wind of it. Salah-ed-Din must have moved like lightning to be here so soon. He probably hopes to draw the King's attention from Beirut. And you, my lady, must leave this town.'

Before Judith could reply, Xenia came from the house, seeming not too disturbed by the news of the Saracen assault. 'Our defenders are all doughty warriors,' she said. 'The enemy will not breach these walls, not in months. But I will send Zebulon to the harbour. One of our ships is loading. It will take your lady and her brother to safety.'

'I shall not go!' Judith exclaimed. 'If there is to be fighting, I am skilled at binding wounds. Will Xenia desert her home? No more shall I leave when my friends are in danger!'

'Send Zebulon,' Geoffrey ordered the merchant's wife, and dragged Judith away into a corner where he stood glowering down at her. 'No one doubts your courage, but if they breach the walls I cannot guarantee your life. I shall stand with the defenders at the walls, and if I am killed there will be no one to protect you.'

'I shall not leave!' Judith vowed. 'If it is all to end here,

I do not care. Edwin will not go home with me. He stays here. Everything I care for is here. Do not make me go, my lord, I beg you.'

For a moment he stared at her questioningly, then turned and strode into the house. Judith followed and found him speaking to Magnus, charging him with her own and Edwin's safety.

'If it seems that the walls will fall, see that you all get to the citadel. You hear me, fellow? If any harm befalls them, you'll answer to me.'

Magnus said nothing, but the proud tilt of his head answered for him and Edwin said fiercely, 'He needs no orders from you to protect us, sir knight. He will give his life without threats from a de Belgarde.'

'Aye—I know that,' Geoffrey said quietly. 'God be with you all.'

He strode past Judith, who stood trembling in the doorway. He would have walked away had she not gone after him, a hand tentatively reaching for his arm. In the middle of the courtyard he stopped and looked round at her with bright, expressionless eyes.

'My lady?'

She withdrew her hand as if he had bitten her, wounded by the polite indifference of his manner. 'I wanted to—to wish you well, sir. Take care of yourself.'

'I am not so foolish as to take unnecessary chances,' he replied. 'And I thank you for your courtesy, even though I know that neither you nor your brother would grieve for the death of a de Belgarde.'

Her blue eyes widened, cloudy with hurt. 'Is that what you believe?'

'You have given me no reason to believe otherwise,'

he said evenly. 'But if you wish to play the part of fond wife let me accommodate you.'

His arms closed round her, drawing her full against the length of his body as his mouth took command of hers. She felt the familiar heat of him through the thin gown she wore, but for once it held no terrors for her. Lifting her hands, she slid her fingers into his hair and pulled his head down to hers, consumed with fears for his safety.

When he released her she stood shaking, trying to stem tears that would not be stemmed. They welled into her eyes, half blinding her, as Geoffrey turned to the gateway. A few moments later she heard the thud of hooves as he rode away to join the defenders at the walls of the town.

The man Zebulon returned with news that Demetrios' ship had already sailed, and all the other merchant ships were loading goods as fast as they could, in order to escape the battle should the Saracens overrun the town. Some of the folk of Jaffa were escaping by sea, too, but most of them had stayed to protect their homes.

It seemed odd to Judith that there was little sign of the siege from Xenia's house by the harbour. Occasionally a trumpet-blast could be heard, or a shout as a hundred men roared all at once at some minor triumph or disaster, but mostly all the evidence was in the wounded men who came, limping or carried on litters, back to the citadel. At night, however, the area round the walls was bright with torchlight and the flare of Greek fire as that awful weapon was flung by either defenders or attackers, to land in pools of flame that could not be extinguished by water.

Magnus and Zebulon had both gone to defend the town, leaving Edwin fretting with youthful fury that he could not go to risk his life, too. Once he tried to join the battle, but when both Judith and Xenia opposed him he threw himself on to the couch and sulked like the little boy he still was in many ways.

It was the third day of the siege when Magnus came running into the house shouting for everyone to make for the citadel.

'They're breaching the walls! They're like madmen! Their siege engines are fearsome. Oh, hurry! To the citadel!'

Grabbing what they could, Judith, Xenia and the two maidservants made haste to obey. They joined the streams of people—mostly women—making for the great walls which protected the citadel, and all the time Magnus kept roaring his warning. 'To the citadel! The walls are down! To the citadel!'

As they pushed and crowded along the streets towards the great gate in the curving walls, a troop of armoured knights rode out, forcing their way through the streams of frightened womenfolk. Judith looked to see if Geoffrey was among them, but their helmets, with the ferocious-looking nose-guard, and the chain-mail drawn up over the lower part of their faces made it impossible to distinguish one from another.

Now the defenders came running for the safety of the citadel and Judith heard faint howls as the Saracen invaders entered the town through the breach where the walls had fallen beneath their onslaught of mining and battering. She found herself crushed against one of Xenia's maids, among a crowd of strangers, with children crying and some of the women in tears. In the panic, she was driven into the heart of the citadel and up to a high room where, eventually, the crush eased.

From the narrow window opening she could see down into the courtyard, which swarmed with armoured men now closing and barring the gate, leaving some of their number to face the maddened charge of the Saracens who raced like a tidal wave through the streets, their swords flashing in the sun as they slashed and stabbed at every living soul they found. Like ants, they found their way into every house, every room, taking anything of value. Casks of wine were trundled out to burst in the streets and add their flow to the blood that ran in the dust. Even the pigs, considered unclean by the Turks, were slaughtered as they ran squealing hither and thither.

Judith turned from the terrible sight, remembering that she had called the Saracens a gentle people and Geoffrey had reminded her that she had not seen them in battle.

Inside the citadel, people huddled in groups, the women and children mostly in the upper rooms while the men remained below. Judith went searching for Edwin and Xenia, finding the merchant's wife in one place and Edwin and Magnus in another. They, at least, were safe. Now her fears were for Geoffrey.

But as she ventured further, to the ground floor and the great hall, the sights she saw—men wounded or horribly burned by Greek fire, some dying silently and others crying aloud—obliged her to stop and offer what help she could. Other women were doing the same, tearing linen into strips to bind the most loathsome of wounds, or using needle and thread to sew up hideous cuts, doing it because this was their part of the war. As she tended the many helpless men, wrapping their hurts and offering wine to soothe dry throats, Judith thought that it was not at all the same as practising on the slashed carcass of a pig in the serene courtyard at Claverham. These were men, suffering pain in greater or lesser degree. All had fought valiantly for three days without rest and now they could smile in gratitude for a kind word and a cool hand on their brow. Even after darkness came she remained among the wounded, picking her way across slumped bodies in the feeble light of torches.

'They want us to surrender,' someone said as she knelt to tend a man whose calf bled profusely.

'Never!' another called, and most echoed the sentiment.

'Surrender to those vile savages?' said the man whose leg Judith was binding. 'Not likely. They ran wild in our streets, did you see?' He looked beyond Judith, saying again, 'Did you see, sir?'

'Yes, I saw,' replied a sombre, familiar voice that made Judith look round with a gasp of relief.

Geoffrey stood there, still clad in mail though he had removed his helmet and the hood-piece of his armour. His cloak hung in shreds, his tunic was streaked with blood, and the skin around his eyes was blackened with sweat and dust, giving that curious gold-green an added lustre.

'Are you wounded?' she asked anxiously.

'I?' he said, frowning as if he had difficulty gathering

his thoughts together. 'No, my lady. I . . . was looking for you. I feared—'

'I, too,' she said, finishing what she was doing before getting to her feet, almost stumbling until Geoffrey caught her hand to support her.

She was unaware of the blood that made her fingers sticky and smudged her gown. His eyes held hers, intense and serious, and his fingers tightened until she felt her bones might break. But she answered the pressure, not caring if he read her heart in her eyes.

'Salah-ed-Din has called for our surrender,' he said, 'but the defenders refuse. The citadel is very strong. It will not fall as easily as the outer walls, but with so many people crushed into one place . . . A lengthy siege will not be pleasant.'

'But if God is with us, we shall survive,' she replied.

'You could have gone free. If you had gone aboard Demetrios' ship . . .'

She shook her head. 'I am glad to be here, to do what I can.'

'And here you must stay,' he said with a sigh. 'Continue your work, my lady. I, too, have duties to attend.'

That night she slept on bare floorboards in common with the rest of the refugees and troops who crowded every inch of space in the citadel. When everyone began to stir with the first light of dawn Judith got up, stretched her aching limbs, and made her way to the stairs, seeking fresh air and more light.

Others had had the same idea. The open rampart of the castle was busy with people, including the leader of the garrison and several of his knights, a few priests, the bishop of Jaffa, and one or two women. As the light increased, Judith saw the havoc in the streets below. Christian corpses lay tossed in piles with the dead pigs; everywhere was evidence of the devastation, in ripped awnings and shattered pottery. And over this carnage flew the Crescent banners of Islam.

Her attention was drawn by a cry from a man who pointed out to sea, where a fleet of over thirty war galleys was approaching the harbour, swift ships with sails a-billow and decks bristling with lances. In the van sailed a proud red ship flying scarlet banners that streamed in the wind, bearing the golden lion of Richard of England.

'The King is come!' someone yelled. 'Spread the word. The Lionheart is with us!'

Judith stood by the parapet with the wind in her hair, watching as the King's ship swept into the harbour a hundred feet below, the fleet not far behind. On the shore a horde of Saracens howled and yelled defiantly. But before the red ship grounded in the shallow water a figure wearing a scarlet surcoat blazoned with lions, a helmet guarding his golden head, leapt from the vessel and plunged shoreward, followed by a shouting band of his barons and men-at-arms. King Richard's sword glinted in the light of the rising sun as he charged straight into the ranks of the enemy, hacking through them as if they were a field of wheat, while each of his ships disgorged its share of warriors to join the fray.

'To the King's aid!' one of the knights cried, and every soldier on the ramparts went plunging down the stairs.

Judith heard the war-cry go up as the gates were undone and the defenders streamed out, given fresh hope and energy by the arrival of their great King. With a stab of dismay, she tried to pick out one figure among that throng of armoured men, though it was impossible. She knew, however, that Geoffrey would be among them.

Other people climbed to the ramparts to watch the battle, including the noble ladies of Jaffa, whose home gave shelter to the refugees.

Before the sun reached the zenith, the town belonged again to the forces of Christendom. As the Saracen army straggled into retreat a great hulloo of triumph from the Crusaders smarted against the ear of every warrior of Islam. The valour of King Richard had defeated his enemies in the very hour of their victory.

Conditions in the town had become so unwholesome that Richard ordered an evacuation of all those under his command. Troops began to set up a tent city outside the walls, for themselves and the women who followed them, but the ladies who had formerly lodged in the citadel—the wives of great lords of Jaffa and the surrounding area—were ordered aboard one of Richard's fleet.

At last Judith saw Geoffrey again and found him unharmed, but her relief turned rapidly to annoyance when he insisted that she, too, should board the ladies' ship, away from the stench of putrefying bodies. He said that Xenia might go with her, but the merchant's wife was anxious to see what damage had been done to her home and her husband's warehouses.

'Then I shall come with you,' Judith said. 'I can help you.'

One look at Geoffrey's face made Xenia shake her

head. 'No, child. You must do as your husband says. I'm used to this sort of thing—it's not the first time we've recovered from a siege. But there's the danger of disease. You can't risk your brother's life. He's not really strong yet.'

For herself Judith would have taken the risk, but not for Edwin. The lad protested bitterly at being sent off with the women, but his pride was salved when Geoffrey gave him a sword and told him it was his duty to protect the ladies—his and Magnus's.

'And you?' Judith asked her husband. 'Where will you be?'

'I stay beside the King,' he replied. 'Go now. The boats are making ready to take you.'

Sore at heart, she trailed between the strutting Edwin and the giant Magnus, casting glances behind her until Geoffrey was hidden from view. Once again he had delegated her to others. She was beginning to feel like a package that no one wanted.

The streets were a terrible sight, littered with dead bodies and broken barrels, the dust turned into mud by the spilled wine and treacherous with shards of broken pottery. Not even the fragrant scent of spices, which pervaded this Eastern land, could cover the awful stench of decaying flesh.

As they approached the harbour where King Richard had landed, Judith saw dead Saracens by the score, their bodies tumbled over one another. She felt sick at the sight and wondered how many more must die before the carnage ended.

There were soldiers everywhere, starting to cart away the dead, and local people exploring the devastation of

their homes. As Judith stood aside to let one of the carts
go past, she met the burning gaze of a woman veiled in
Arab black. Those flashing dark eyes seemed familiar,
so filled with hatred that Judith felt seared by their blaze.
But before she could believe her senses the woman had
darted past, on her way towards the citadel, her
bracelets jingling.

'Another whore,' Edwin said. 'She'll be plying her
trade in the camp tonight. The men will be ready for a
little fun after all the fighting. Come, Sister.'

He laid a heavy hand on her arm, but she wrenched
free, crying, 'Why do men think they may lead me
everywhere I have to go? I shall not go to the ship!'

'You'll do as you're told,' her brother said, taking
fresh hold of her with a strength she had not guessed he
possessed. 'It's for your safety.'

She allowed herself to be taken to the shore, to the
rowing boat that waited. Though she told herself the
veiled woman could have been anyone she knew with
awful certainty that she had seen Mariamne. Mariamne,
here in Jaffa, looking for Geoffrey.

The girl must be mad to have risked coming among the
enemy on her own, but it was the madness of love,
single-minded and blind to danger. Any man would
respond to such evidence of a woman's devotion, and
Geoffrey was human—all too human. It took little
imagination to know how he would spend his night.

CHAPTER
NINE

WHILE parties of men set about cleaning and rebuilding the town, the ship carrying the ladies anchored outside the harbour, from where they could see the tented encampment of King Richard's army. Small boats came out bringing fresh fruit and every kind of comfort, but for Judith the two days that followed were filled with doubts and misery.

The ladies of Jaffa had lived in Palestine all of their lives and had adopted the flowing muslin gowns of the natives. They painted their faces with rouge and kohl, decked themselves in bangles, and walked with a mincing gait more fitted to women of the harem than to the great-grand-daughters of Vikings. Finding that Judith was a relative newcomer, they amused themselves in outfitting her with filmy clothes and ornaments. She allowed herself to be fashioned into a facsimile of themselves, for she thought that this, perhaps, was what attracted the men of Outremer. Certainly Geoffrey had found Mariamne attractive with her black-rimmed eyes and sensuous walk.

Mariamne—the thought of the Saracen princess tormented her.

Even from the deck of the ship many women could be seen in the camp and Judith was not surprised to learn that prostitutes openly plied their wares among the army—that was one reason why the ladies would not venture ashore to visit their lords: only women of low virtue walked freely where so many common soldiers would leer at them. Was Mariamne among them, waiting her chance to see Geoffrey? Or .was she with him, warming his bed?

On the third morning of their incarceration on the ship, Judith rose as usual at dawn, washed her hands and face and donned a loose gown of lilac muslin over her linen chemise. Barely was she dressed when a shout from the watchman drew all the ladies from behind their curtains on the deck.

The hills beyond the encampment bristled with Saracen soldiers, a dark mass of footmen and mounted troops advancing on the Christian army.

'They're making a surprise attack!' Edwin cried as trumpets rang out from among the tents and the camp city came alive with scrambling men dragging on clothes and armour. 'Come, Magnus! To the fray!'

To Judith's horror, her brother grabbed his sword and jumped over the ship's side into the shallow water of low tide, the giant serf following. Together, the two waded to the beach and ran to join the army as it gathered itself hastily to meet the screaming onslaught of the enemy.

From where she stood, Judith could see the end of the curving defensive line which had been hurriedly thrown into being. Behind piles of baggage, spearmen knelt with lances butted into the ground to ward off the attacking horsemen, and behind them a line of bow-men stood with arrows notched and crossbows spitting deadly bolts, and behind them again a second line of soldiers waited to reload and draw a second wave of bows.

Twice the Saracen cavalry thundered in and twice they were beaten off in a hail of arrows, but the third time a bold group braved the uncertain footing of the sand dunes and swept round the end of the defensive lines to engage in hand-to-hand combat with Crusaders who ran eagerly to repulse them.

Judith saw Magnus, unmistakable because of his huge stature and flaming hair. He speared one horseman and unseated another with a blow from an axe, then he was lost to sight in the mêlée of horses and clanging weapons. One by one the incursers fell, until only a single one of their number remained. He tried to get back across the dunes, but his way was barred by the red-bearded serf, who swung his axe again—and fell as the curved Saracen sword slashed his throat. A moment later, the Turk fell, too, cut down by a fierce assault from three foot-soldiers.

Stricken by the sight of Magnus's death, Judith found herself unable to look away as a fresh wave of cavalry attacked the lines and in places skirmishes broke out as the wall of spearmen broke momentarily. But each time the enemy charged through they met a ferocious reply from the Crusaders, the line reformed, and the Saracen cavalry withdrew.

Eventually there came a lull. The enemy had charged time and time again only to be beaten off with the loss of many lives. The brazen clamour of trumpets rang round the hills, recalling the decimated squadrons of horse-men.

'Now the foot-soldiers will attack,' one of the ladies said. 'Pray God my lord is safe.'

And mine, Judith thought fervently, and my brother. Ever since she had seen Magnus fall she had been watching for Edwin's fair head, but in vain. Magnus had been his protector all his life. Without the serf, Edwin was defenceless. She waited, scarcely daring to breathe, for the expected charge of thousands of howling enemy infantry.

But the foot-soldiers did not advance. A strange hush fell over the battlefield and even the wind had died as if it, too, held its breath. At last, incredibly, Judith saw that the Turks were in retreat. That whole vast army had turned and was marching away, disappearing among the hills.

A shout of victory rose from the embattled camp—and out from the town came a rowing boat bringing melons and dates for the refreshment of the ladies.

The general mood was one of rejoicing; it had been a famous victory for the forces of Christendom, who had beaten off the might of Saladin's army even though it had almost caught them sleeping. The Crusader lines had withstood and triumphed, because Richard of England had put heart into his men by his own personal courage and by his very presence among them. Or so the minstrels would sing.

But for Judith, fears for those she loved overcame the sense of triumph. Magnus was dead, Edwin vanished. And Geoffrey?

Some of the other ladies shared her unease, but one by

one messages came, or the lords themselves took time to visit the ship and reassure their wives. None of them had been seriously hurt, though they had been caught unawares and some of them had fought without armour, having had no time for donning mail.

'Mistress Judith!' one of the ladies called as she stood beside a stocky, gnarled man. 'Judith, my lord has a message for you.'

Judith curtseyed to the man, whom she knew to be Baron Guy of Jaffa, and looked hopefully into his round, unsmiling face. 'My lord? Sir Geoffrey de Belgarde—is he—'

'He is wounded,' Baron Guy said gravely. 'He took a lance in the shoulder and has lost much blood, I fear.' Seeing Judith turn pale, he touched her arm as if to comfort her. 'Nay, don't worry. He will recover, I dare say. I spoke with him myself. He asked me to tell you that your brother is unharmed—I saw the lad myself. Sir Geoffrey wants him to join you here, but your brother seems unwilling.'

Relief brought a little colour back to her cheeks. 'He will be difficult, I know. My lord . . . may I visit my husband? To see with my own eyes . . .'

'He said you were not to come,' he replied, rubbing his chin thoughtfully. 'An army camp is no place for a lady. But if you will allow me to escort you I can see you safely there, and back. Were I wounded, I would wish to have the comfort of my wife's presence. And perhaps you can persuade your brother to be reasonable. He's young, and gently-born. He should be training for knighthood, not rubbing shoulders with the common ranks.'

'Thank you, my lord,' Judith said fervently, dipping another deep curtsey.

She waited impatiently until Baron Guy had finished his visit with his wife, then she drew a mantle over her muslin gown and went with him to the rowing boat which had brought him.

In the encampment, she saw why the ladies would not venture there—women in the sheerest of clothes paraded with swinging hips and the common soldiers appeared to have forgotten all decency, using the foulest of language, some of them even tumbling the gaudily-dressed women in full view of their panting fellows. Judith averted her eyes and was glad when they reached the colourful tents of the nobility. There horses were being curried and arms sharpened, while knights and barons talked over the day's victory. She was the object of more than one pair of curious, admiring eyes as she walked beside lord Guy, who stepped up to one of the tents and drew back the flap.

'Sir Geoffrey?' he called. 'I've brought you a welcome visitor. I'll give you a few minutes with her, then I'll escort her back.'

In the dimness of the tent, Judith made out a low divan where Geoffrey lay propped up on silk cushions, stripped to the waist with a thick wadding round his shoulder and his arm in a sling. She walked slowly across the trodden grass to a rug beside the bed, but there was no welcome in her husband's face, only a grim tautness that quenched her spirits.

'You should not have come,' he said.

'I wanted to. I wanted to see—'

'Whether I was dying or not?' he broke in, his voice

clipped with bitterness. 'Nay, lady, your prayers have
gone unanswered yet again.'

'I have been praying for your safety!' she cried, and
sank to her knees beside him, pleading with him. 'Oh, let
me stay. You need someone to nurse you.'

'I shall not be here for long,' he replied. 'The King will
need me. But the fleet will be leaving for Acre. You go
with it and wait for me there. Attend on the Queen until
I come for you.'

'You're always sending me away,' Judith said dully.
'How can you return to your duties when you are sorely
wounded?'

'Sorely, but not mortally.'

'Sir, for once pray think of your own safety! There
must be others who could act as envoy. What point is
there in risking your life when all the talking does no
good? The war still goes on.'

Sighing, Geoffrey slid further down on the cushions,
looking up at the swaying roof of the tent. 'The Saracens
are as weary of fighting as we are, and the King wants to
be gone. This time terms will be found for a truce.'

'And must you be one of the ambassadors?' she asked,
watching his face, seeing it drawn with pain and loss of
blood.

'I must. Would you have me leave off now, when an
end is within reach? You do not understand.'

'I understand well enough. You wish to be rid of me.
You wish to stay here with—'

He turned his head, his eyes clouded with pain and
puzzlement. 'With whom?'

Looking down at her hands, Judith muttered, 'With
the King.'

'Nay, lady, that is not what you meant.' His good hand came out and touched her shoulder, his fingers pressing her flesh. 'With whom?'

'The Princess Mariamne.'

Geoffrey laughed shortly, the sound cut off in a wince of pain. 'She is safe in Megiddo. I shall not see her again.'

'She was in Jaffa three days ago,' she told him quietly, lifting her eyes to his. 'Disguised in Arab robes and veil. I saw her as I went down to the harbour.' When she saw the swift dismay that showed in his face, she wished the words unsaid, but it was too late to retract them.

'Mariamne here?' he said under his breath. 'You must be mistaken.'

'I only wish I were. She must have run away to find you, el-Asad.' Bitterness had crept into her voice as she spoke the foreign name, for she was sure that it was Mariamne who had named him Mountain Lion—a name bestowed with pride, and with love. Of that she had no doubt. 'Her people will think her disgraced, will they not? She has thrown away everything for your sake. You must make sure her sacrifice is not in vain. Soon I shall be gone from Outremer, with or without my brother, and you will be free, sir.'

'God's eyes!' he got out, trying to sit up, but the effort proved too much and he sank back with a groan, sweat beading his forehead. 'She should not have taken such a risk. I must find her at once.'

'Aye, sir, find her. Perhaps the bishop of Jaffa will grant you a swift annulment and baptise her at the same time. If that occurs, pray send me word. I shall wish to know whether I am wife or maid.'

Before he could reply, a shaft of sunlight widened as the tent-flap was pulled back and Baron Guy's voice said, 'I fear I must interrupt, mistress Judith. I've found your brother to take you back to the ship.'

She looked round, seeing Edwin's lanky figure, hair shining fair in the sunlight, beside the muscular Guy of Jaffa.

'I shall come at once,' she said, turning back to Geoffrey. With the increased light she could better see the sickly pallor which underlay his sun-browned skin, and his eyes that still flung taunts at her. She leaned forward and placed a kiss on his damp brow, saying low-voiced, 'Goodbye, my husband. God keep you,' and with her eyes averted she rose and left the tent, her pain too deep for tears.

Her dearest wish would have been to stay beside Geoffrey and tend him as a wife should, nursing him to make sure he recovered from the grievous wound, but that was not possible. Her love for Geoffrey was a hopeless thing. She felt that she would not care if her life ended.

Edwin regarded her from his eye-corners, his lower lip set in the sulky fashion she had come to detest, but Baron Guy laid a hand on his shoulder as if to encourage him.

'Off with you, lad. Get her back to the ship before night falls. Farewell, Judith of Claverham.'

'And you, my lord,' she replied. 'Thank you for your help.'

She trailed behind Edwin, her eyes alert for any woman robed in black, but there were many of them, laundry-women and drudges, and others brightly-clad in garments that revealed swelling breasts as they walked with provocative gait among the appreciative soldiers. Judith saw no sign of Mariamne.

The rowing boat which had brought her from the ship lay waiting on the edge of the sea, its boatman half-asleep in the late sunlight. To Judith's dull surprise, Edwin stopped a little way up the beach, waving her on.

'But—you are coming with me,' she said.

Her brother made a negative gesture. 'I have been offered a place among the King's retainers. One of his squires is sick. I shall stay with the King until he comes to Acre, sister. Wait for me there. Before we meet again I shall have decided what to do. But one thing is sure—I shall not go back to Castle Belgarde while Earl Torquil lives. Because of him, Magnus is dead. Magnus was my friend.'

'I know,' she said softly, seeing the tears that welled in her brother's blue eyes before he turned and walked away. Judith watched him go, aware of the subtle change that had come over him. This final battle, and the death of Magnus, had brought him nearer to maturity, taken away the sulky stubbornness and replaced it with the strength of resolution.

For herself, she felt she had lost everything—her brother, her husband. All that remained was the Priory, waiting to enclose her in a wimple and habit in a world of plainsong and prayer behind the locked door of the cloister.

When the fleet sailed for Acre, Judith went with it, back to the Queen's apartments in the citadel of that busy port, where the ladies awaited the final return of their menfolk.

'I shall be glad to leave this fly-ridden land,' Lady Joan declared, rapidly wafting a fan that stirred her white veil. 'In summer it is too hot, and in winter it rains so much the land is churned to mud. Oh, for the seasons of England! Pray God we get there while autumn colours the land. My brother John will have to look to himself when Richard returns. Richard will be welcomed like a hero.'

'As he deserves,' Queen Berengaria said loyally. 'They say at Jaffa he excelled himself. He rode between the lines challenging all comers to single combat, but there were none who dared accept. The Saracens fear him more than any knight in Christendom.'

'I heard,' Lady Joan added, 'that when his horse was killed by an arrow the Sultan himself sent out a fresh mount for him. Did you see it, Judith?'

Judith, sewing by the window embrasure where a soft breeze came from the sea, lifted her heavy head to reply, 'No, my lady. We could not see the heart of the battle. But it sounds the kind of courtesy that the Sultan would offer.'

'Hah!' Lady Joan exclaimed. 'You claim personal knowledge of Saladin, do you?'

'No, my lady,' Judith said. The true story of her sojourn in Megiddo could never be told. Best to keep her counsel rather than face the scorn of the sharp-tongued Lady Joan.

Lost in memories, she touched the hard outline of the opal she wore against her skin—not because it held tender associations but because the servants in the citadel were not to be trusted; the sight of such a gem might have proved too tempting for their light fingers. Even so, she wondered if it might not have been better for her to be incarcerated in Hasan's harem, tended by slaves, bathed and perfumed daily, dressed in the wondrous clothes the Turkish ladies wore, and now and then being wooed by the handsome dark-eyed emir. 'You shall lie against silk pillows and I shall adore you,' he had promised.

But handsome as Hasan was, the thought of his touching her made her shudder. The only man she wanted was Geoffrey de Belgarde, and he was as distant as the moon. He loved Mariamne and that love was returned. By now he must have found her and, probably, he would take her to Xenia's house for protection. Comfortless as the possibility was, it was better than the alternative—that his wound had festered in the heat. To think of him with Mariamne was bitter gall, but to think of him dead was unbearable.

Eventually, a page brought a message—the Lady Judith was wanted in the great hall by a person who had been asking for her.

'Well, well,' Lady Joan said drily. 'Your recalcitrant husband has returned at last. Truly he is ardent in his need of you.'

On an earlier occasion, Judith had flown to meet Geoffrey, but this time she went on reluctant feet to learn her fate. Was the marriage annulled? Would he say that Mariamne had been converted and would become his wife?

A few knights and their squires lazed in the great hall, idly playing with the dogs that padded across the straw beneath rafters blackened by smoke, while servants hurried about their chores. Judith glanced around for a man dressed in the uniform of St John, but to her great anxiety it was Edwin who came to meet her. Edwin, arrayed in a fine linen tunic and cloak, his pale hair neatly cut and his shoulders set proudly.

Fearing the worst, Judith managed, 'What news of Sir Geoffrey?'

'Your husband is well,' her brother replied in a lofty tone. 'At least, he is recovering his strength—enough to play messenger-boy to the King again.'

Judith eyed him with distaste. 'Sarcasm sits ill on you, Edwin. I know that you hate his father, but Sir Geoffrey has never wished you harm. He is a good man.'

'Perhaps so,' he conceded, examining a torn finger-nail.

'Is there—is there a woman with him?' she got out through a thickness in her throat.

Edwin's eyes snapped back to her face, narrowing. 'A woman? I thought you trusted him, sister. I doubt he has time for dalliance, being so involved in the peace talks. But I did not come to discuss your husband. I have news—I am to join the household of Lord Guy of Jaffa.'

The announcement held no surprise for her. She only dimly heard it, for her mind was on Geoffrey. Obviously Edwin knew very little about her husband, probably had only heard his name mentioned now and then. So if he had, discreetly, taken up with the Turkish princess it was likely that Edwin might not have known of it.

'I must thank you for bringing me to his notice,' her brother was saying. 'He has promised to train me in the skills of knighthood and when I am of age he may grant me a manor of my own, here in Outremer. With the revenues from Claverham I shall be a wealthy man some day.'

'I trust it will be so,' she replied.

Impulsively, becoming again the boy she had known, Edwin grasped her hand. 'We shall not quarrel, you and I. Some day I may be able to give you a dowry—a small one, but even so as your brother it will be my duty to see you cared for. Meanwhile, Lord Guy asks me to say that you would be welcome to stay with his lady and wait on her, until Sir Geoffrey finds some fortune of his own. You may stay here in Outremer, Judith.'

'I cannot.' She withdrew her hand from his clasp, seeing his crestfallen look. 'I am glad for you, Edwin, but I must go home—to the Priory. My marriage is to be annulled. It was never a real marriage. It was forced upon us both, under circumstances that I cannot explain now. You see, there was no plot.'

He stared at her with bewildered eyes as blue as her own. 'It was not done because of Earl Torquil?'

'No, it was not! How can you believe such a thing of me, Edwin? You have known me all your life. Who taught you to play fivestones, and chess? Do you think your own sister capable of plotting for your death?'

'No,' he said with a sorrowful shake of his head. 'But when I was at Castle Belgarde the Earl made me believe . . . Judith, forgive me! When I learned you had come after me—and then to discover you married to the Earl's son . . . It seemed like a plot. I was confused. Please—' He took her hand again, holding it to his breast. 'I beseech you to forgive me, sister. You have no idea how the Earl can twist a man's mind, making him believe

things he does not want to believe. I thought you had
turned against me, too. That is partly why I ran away. I
felt so alone! But since Sir Geoffrey saved my life I have
wondered if I might be wrong.'

'He—saved your life?' she queried. 'When?'

'Outside Jaffa, in the thick of that last battle. Did he
not tell you? I felt sure he would tell you.'

'A true knight does not boast of his own bravery!'

Edwin had the grace to look down in shame, colour
staining his cheeks. 'You are right. But it did happen,
sister. I would be dead, were it not for Sir Geoffrey de
Belgarde, much as it pains me to admit it.'

'Is that how he got his wound?' she breathed.

'Aye, it is.' His eyes met hers again. 'After I saw
Magnus cut down I was so overcome with grief that I
threw myself into the nearest mêlée, wanting to kill
every Saracen in sight. I was so wild with madness that I
forgot my own safety. A horseman came at me with a
lance. I did not see him until the last moment. Then I was
hurled aside—by Sir Geoffrey. He took the lance in his
own shoulder. He was without armour. The attack came
so suddenly that the knights had not time to put on all
their mail. Some of them fought half-naked. Sir Geoffrey . . . fell at my feet. Others killed the horseman. My
brain was so thick with battle-madness that I did not
comprehend, at first. He saved my life, Judith, when my
death would have given him Claverham. Why did he do
that?'

'Because he is a true and honourable knight,' Judith
said.

She saw now that Edwin was a headstrong youth, but
he could be forgiven his mistakes. Under Baron Guy's

patronage, she felt sure, her brother would develop into a knight worthy of his spurs.

After he had gone, she kept reliving the scene he had described—of the battlefield and Geoffrey's selfless courage. Such a deed was final proof that Geoffrey did not share his father's evil ambitions and she loved him the more because of it. With Edwin she had found an understanding, but every day that passed only made her more sorrowful over her coming parting with her husband.

While the peace discussions continued in earnest, contingents of the army slowly made their way back to Acre, bringing news of the negotiations and gossip that was sometimes amusing and sometimes shocking, but always of interest to the bored Lady Joan. She would be off chatting to one or another of the barons and return to the bower to regale her companions with anecdotes. But a day dawned when her amusement was spiked with spite—spite directed at Judith.

'Your handsome husband has disgraced himself, it seems, mistress Judith,' Lady Joan said with a high-pitched laugh. 'Come, ladies, listen to this! Sir Geoffrey de Belgarde—that fine knight of St John—the King's favourite envoy—and lover of Infidels . . .'

The list might have been extended had not the Queen put in softly, 'Lady Joan, you overreach yourself. Sir Geoffrey is respected by all who know him. If you have some news to impart, pray tell us in a seemly manner, without this embroidery of rhetoric.'

'Forgive me,' Lady Joan said, but she was not contrite. Her eyes still sparkled as she gazed around the faces of her listeners, reserving a particularly gleeful look for Judith. 'But the gossip is juicy as a well-ripened fig and I can scarce contain myself. Sir Geoffrey may well have been respected, but now there is a blot on his escutcheon which will not be forgotten for a long time. Involved in a brawl, he was—a brawl with a common foot-soldier—over a whore!'

Judith turned white to the lips, her eyes wide with pain, and the Queen sent her a sympathetic look, saying, 'Have a care, Lady Joan. Such talk may damage a man's reputation.'

'But it is true! I heard it from the lips of the Earl of Leicester, who had it from Sir Guarin of Harfleur, who was present at the scene. Sir Geoffrey flew into such a jealous rage that he killed the unfortunate man where he stood. And the woman, as it it turned out, was a Turk! A fine knight, indeed! He slew an inferior, over a houri, like any base-born villain.'

In the ensuing silence, Judith stared down at the piece of embroidery she had been working on, aware that all eyes had turned to her. She would not have believed the tale to be true, except for one thing—the woman had been a Turk. But not a whore—that part of the rumour must be muddled.

So they were together, Geoffrey and his princess, and by his action he had shown the world his possessive interest in her.

'Does the King know of this?' Berengaria asked.

'He does,' Lady Joan replied. 'But it seems he absolved his favourite of all blame. The soldier, so it was said, drew a knife on Sir Geoffrey, and they called the subsequent killing self-defence. Self-defence! A knight's sword against a foot-soldier's puny knife. But the King was always blind where Sir Geoffrey de Belgarde was concerned.'

'And you, Lady Joan,' the Queen said in a quiet voice that yet managed to contain censure, 'were always too aware of him as a man. Is this scorn summoned by your disappointment?'

The King's sister turned an unlovely shade of puce before she stormed from the bower in a fury, but Judith guessed there was truth in the Queen's assertion. She was comforted, just a little, to understand at last why she had been the target for Lady Joan's verbal darts ever since Geoffrey had first brought her to the bower. Lady Joan wanted him for herself, but presumably he had failed to respond. No woman stood a chance with him—except the Sultan Saladin's sloe-eyed niece.

CHAPTER
TEN

KING Richard Coeur de Lion returned to Acre amid
fanfares of trumpets, the people turning out to cheer him
through the streets. At last a peace had been sealed: the
coast of Palestine, from Tyre to Jaffa, was to remain in
Christian hands and, though Jerusalem itself still came
under the sway of Islam, pilgrims were free to visit the
city and its shrines without hindrance, and traders could
now travel freely between the lands of Saladin and the
principalities of Christendom. Indeed, many pilgrims
had already set out for the Holy City. It was a triumph of
diplomacy if not quite the overwhelming victory of
which King Richard had dreamed.

Judith heard the trumpets and the cheering as she sat
alone in the bower, unable to take part in the rejoicing.
For her, the end of the war meant the end of her stay in
the Holy Land—the end of her marriage to Geoffrey de
Belgarde. All she could hope for was a swift departure
with as little pain as possible. She would have to see
Geoffrey, of course, but she intended the meeting to be
calm and dignified. Not for anything would she have him
guess that her heart was dead within her.

What she had not expected was to have Geoffrey burst
into the bower without even the courtesy of a knock. She
was on her feet, exclaiming in outrage, before she fully

registered the identity of the tall knight in the long striped robe and dark cloak. Her protests trailed off into silence as she stared at him. He still looked ill, hollows in his cheeks and his skin paler than she had seen it, but those dark-fringed eyes flashed with their old fire, throwing out a challenge.

'What, sulking alone, my lady?' he demanded. 'Why are you not with the rest, making merry?'

'I—I felt unwell,' she said truthfully enough, though her indisposition was of the spirit rather than the flesh. 'Sir, why have you come uninvited here? If I had not been alone—'

'I made sure you were alone before I came. Lady Elena told me where I might find you. And you are my wife, are you not?'

She lowered her eyes, unable to bear looking at him when she must not love him or care that he looked so changed by his illness. 'Aye, for the moment. What news do you bring?'

'The war is over. The peace is signed. What better news do you wish for? Your brother is settled in Jaffa, and content with his lot. And I am recovered.'

'Are you?' Forcing herself, she looked up, her eyes clouded.

He grimaced. 'Almost. There is a lingering weakness caused by loss of blood, but with rest I shall be well again soon enough. And you—what is the cause of your paleness?'

'Anyone would grow pale waiting here for men to decide her fate,' she said with a touch of bitterness. 'When am I to leave, sir? Have you had time to arrange passage for me yet?'

For a moment he was silent, watching her thoughtfully. 'Are you so anxious to be gone, my lady?'

'I shall be glad to be quit of this land,' Judith said, turning away from him to stare out of the window at the sea.

'Very well.' The words came quietly, on the breath of a sigh. 'Then I shall arrange it as soon as I may. You will wish to be in England before the winter storms begin.'

'It would be as well.' She clenched her hand at her breast, feeling the shape of the opal as she struggled to control her emotions, but the wild mixture of pain, love and bitter jealousy made her head throb so much that she laid it against the cold stone of the embrasure, her eyes tight-closed to deny the tears that threatened. Why did he stay here torturing her? Why could he not have done with it and leave? Surely he was anxious to be gone—back to Mariamne's entwining arms?

'The King may take a few weeks before he leaves,' Geoffrey said in a colourless tone. 'Will you travel with the Queen?'

'No!' She swung round, her head swimming. 'I want to go now. Soon.'

His face was as expressionless as his voice and he seemed paler than ever, making her near frantic with concern. 'As you will, my lady. I shall see to it.'

As he turned to the door, she perversely did not want him to go. 'Do you know that people are talking about you?' she got out raggedly. 'Talking. Laughing. Was it necessary to behave like a moon-struck calf? You always took pride in your good name. Why did you throw it away?'

A deep line appeared between his brows as he

frowned. 'You speak in riddles, my lady. What slander is being spread about me?'

'Don't you know?'

'Nay, I do not.'

She flung a hand to her head, fearing that it might burst. How could he deny knowing about the gossip that had started? He must know—unless the tale were untrue. Grasping at the faint hope, she said, 'They say you killed a man, in a brawl.'

The frown changed, becoming tinged with regret. 'Aye, so I did. With good reason.'

Bitter laughter jerked out of her. 'You call it good reason—to sully your honour in a street-fight with a common foot-soldier? But of course she was not any woman, was she? And she would have done the same for you—she would have murdered me. Now you have committed murder for her. What did the poor man do—look at her? Could you not even bear to have another man lay eyes on her?'

He let out a wordless snarl of rage and advanced on her, swinging her round against the wall with such force that dizziness made her vision blur. His face was a dark mass in front of her, very close to her, as he growled, 'Murder, madam? Is that what they are saying? Is that what you believe? Great and good God, will you never cease to insult me?' Hard hands on her shoulders shook her without mercy until the tears burst from her eyes; then he stepped away, looking coldly at her as she leaned weakly against the wall. 'Get your mantle, madam. You are coming with me.'

'To where?' she croaked.

'To wherever I choose to take you, wife! Get your

mantle, or by God I swear I shall carry you from this room across my shoulder and give the court something more to chew on.'

Not daring to argue, she took down her blue mantle from the pole where it hung. She was afraid now, for she had seen him angry before but never quite this angry, with the bitter, icy fury of a blizzard. As she fastened the mantle, Geoffrey seized her wrist and dragged her to the door, ignoring her cry of pain as his fingers bit into her bones.

What did he intend to do with her? she wondered, half-dazed with fright as he led her down the stairs and across the end of the great hall. One or two among the gathered throng stopped talking to stare and break into curious whispers that Judith knew would spread with the ease of a flood across flat land, reaching every ear in the citadel. How amused Lady Joan would be!

In the courtyard, he forced her across to the stables, where he ordered two horses to be saddled—one with a leading-rein—and while grooms hurried to obey he stood black-faced with rage, his hand still locked about her wrist so tightly that it almost stopped the flow of blood. She could feel her fingers going numb.

'Geoffrey, please!' she breathed, trying to unlock the brutal grip. 'Where are we going?'

He ignored her, not even looking at her. In the sunlight his face looked gaunt, his handsome profile seeming carved from unfeeling stone, and around his mouth a rim of white betokened his grim fury.

Under the curious sidelong stares of the grooms and stable-boys, Judith found herself mounting a grey palfrey, waiting there in apprehension as her husband leapt onto a tall chestnut stallion and, taking her leading rein in one hand, he rode towards the great gate of the citadel.

They passed through the streets of Acre, by the thronged bazaar, unnoticed by the crowds who chattered merrily, sellers crying their wares, tumblers tumbling for the amusement of those who enjoyed the holiday atmosphere of newly-made peace in the land. Judith glimpsed a lion in a cage, staring balefully at those who crowded to gape at him as though he would leap at them and tear them apart but for the bars that contained him. Glancing sidelong at Geoffrey, she saw the same wild fury raging within him, ready to savage her if his self-control slipped. Mountain Lion, she thought, and jealousy blazed within her anew.

'Where are you taking me?' she said desperately as they approached the gates of the town.

He flung her a bleak, glittering look. 'Where we shall settle this matter once and for all time, lady,' he answered, which was no answer at all. What did he mean? But his chill distance prevented her from asking.

Once beyond the walls of the town, Geoffrey spurred his mount to a gallop, obliging Judith to keep pace as her palfrey struggled to obey the hard hand on its leading rein. A warm wind tore at her hair, threatening to dislodge her veil and unravel the careful braids as it tossed her mantle behind her. They rode through yellow hills, past crags that threw long shadows as the sun sank behind them.

After a while, Judith saw the green of an oasis ahead, where bright tents had been erected beneath palm trees. Horses were tethered and men took their ease, sitting on the ground as they conversed—Saracens, every one of them. Geoffrey rode to where the other horses browsed in the grass beside a deep, cool pool of water, and there he drew rein.

A puzzled Judith saw one of the seated men detach himself from the group and come strolling towards her, throwing out his arms in welcome. To her surprise, she recognised Hasan.

He seemed more subdued than usual, more serious, as he watched Geoffrey dismount. 'El-Asad, my friend,' he said gravely. 'I am glad to see you.'

'And I to be here,' Geoffrey replied.

The two men shook hands with great solemnity, exchanging a long, meaningful look; then Hasan was smiling up at Judith. 'Welcome, Lady of the Moon, to the Oasis of Friendship.'

Speaking in Turkish, Geoffrey said something which made the other man look round at him. Hasan replied in the same language, and glanced back at Judith with a gleam in his eye, as if whatever Geoffrey had said had caused him inner amusement, though Geoffrey looked as severe as ever.

'May I help your lady down?' Hasan enquired.

'Aye, do so,' Geoffrey replied. 'My shoulder is stiff.'

The Saracen prince held out his arms invitingly, hiding his smile in his black beard. Wondering what mischief was afoot, Judith looked uncertainly at her husband. The ways of Muslims were a mystery to her. Was there to be an exchange—herself for Mariamne? Surely not!

'Well, dismount, lady!' Geoffrey said brusquely. 'Do not keep the emir waiting.'

'He has given me his permission,' Hasan reminded her with a twinkle and took her by the waist, lifting her from the saddle with consummate ease and setting her safely on the ground. He released her immediately, only to bow low over her hand. 'How fortunate my friend is in his wife,' he murmured. 'Were I your husband, I too would choose to marry only one woman.'

Having been reprimanded before for being too friendly with Hasan, Judith chose not to reply apart from inclining her head in acknowledgement of the compliment. But she sensed a new understanding between the men, which lacked the bristling hostility of earlier encounters. Had the signing of the peace treaty made such a difference to their personal enmity, or was there some other cause?

'Please follow me,' Hasan said, leading the way to a tent set a little apart from the rest, a large square structure of billowing scarlet cloth, where he paused to draw aside the flap and smile again at Judith.

'This tent has been prepared for your use. El-Asad must rest. Even a Mountain Lion has need of relaxation when he is recovering from a wound, and in your company he may regain his full strength, Lady of the Moon. My slaves will attend to your needs. You will find garments—gifts from my wives to the wife of my friend. I wish you both peace and joy, al-Khatun, el-Asad. May Allah smile on you while you remain with us.'

Geoffrey replied in Turkish and the men exchanged formal bows before Hasan departed, an erect and dignified figure in his turban and flowing robes.

'What is this?' Judith said stiffly. 'Do you mock me, sir? To bring me here when you know—'

'It would have been churlish to refuse Hasan's generous offer,' Geoffrey replied. 'I had no wish to offend him.'

'And must we play games in order not to offend him? You surely do not expect me to stay here with you when—'

'You will stay!' he interrupted, grasping her arm to thrust her into the shadowy interior of the tent.

Stumbling on the edge of a carpet, Judith sprawled to her knees, her senses quickening to the scent of incense which rose from a burner. Cushions covered in bright silks strewed the carpet around a low table, and a broad divan covered in furs stood invitingly, draped with muslin curtains to keep out the flies. Appalled, Judith looked round at her husband, who stood over her with his feet planted apart, his thumbs hooked into the sword-belt which girded the striped robe over a shirt and linen trousers. Had he been bearded, he would have looked like a Saracen himself, a dark and dangerous man with the tawny-green eyes of a great cat.

'I do not understand,' she said in a voice that shook. 'Why have you brought me here, sir? To humiliate me? We are not properly wed—there were no Christian witnesses to the ceremony. You swore you would seek an annulment.'

Geoffrey folded his arms, looking down across them as she knelt at his feet. 'Perhaps I have changed my mind.'

The breath caught in her throat, for she saw no softness in his face, only the cold disdain of a master in whose power she was helpless. 'You cannot! Sir, this must be a cruel jest! It is not me you want. Or—' Her eyes widened as the thought struck her with awful realisation. 'Does Hasan know his sister ran away to find you? Is this mummery intended to mislead him?'

'Hasan knows everything,' he replied in an even tone.

'Then why does he treat you as his friend?'

'Because *he* had the grace to listen to the truth and believe it.'

Struggling with a feeling of unreality, as if she were dreaming, she laid a hand to her head. 'What truth? Mariamne was with you. Do you deny she was the woman over whom you fought—the woman for whom you killed a man?'

'No, I do not deny it. That is the truth—or part of it. Now you will do me the courtesy of listening to the rest.'

Giving her another bleak look, he walked slowly to the divan, threw back the thin curtain and sat down, weariness etched in every line of him as he eased his wounded shoulder. Judith longed to go to him, to fold her arms about him and bid him rest, but she reminded herself that it was Mariamne he wanted. What had happened between them? Had the princess gone back to her own people? Was this tent Hasan's way of compensating his friend, in the hope that Judith would make Geoffrey forget his real love?

It would be hard to be second best, she thought sadly, but it would be better than nothing.

'The Princess Mariamne was in Jaffa,' Geoffrey said quietly, head bent and his gaze on the patterned carpet as he leaned on his knees. 'Where she stayed I do not know. Perhaps she sought me, but we did not meet. After I was wounded, I took ill with a fever and had no chance to look for her, but when I regained my senses I made enquiries. She was nowhere to be found.'

'But you did find her!' Judith exclaimed, consumed by jealousy as she recognised the sorrow in him.

A spasm of anger crossed his face and his mouth tightened. 'Yes. Eventually. I was walking through the camp when I heard her call my name. It was dark, and I saw her struggling on the ground with a man who behaved like an animal. Her clothes were torn, her person violated. When I dragged the man from her he came at me with a knife in his drunken rage and I ran him through. I would have done the same to any foul creature who would rape a helpless woman.'

Unable to face the bright glitter in his eyes, she looked at the hands she was twisting in her lap. 'Then the rumours were untrue. It was not dishonourable. Forgive me, sir.'

'There's more,' he said hoarsely. 'Mariamne knelt at my feet weeping in her distress. She said she was no longer worthy of me, or of her people. Before I could prevent her, she had taken the knife which the vile creature dropped and plunged it into her breast. She died in my arms.'

She lifted her head, stunned by the news he spoke in such flat tones that she guessed the pain it caused him. 'Geoffrey . . .'

'I took her body back to Megiddo,' he went on, his gaze locked with hers. 'It was done secretly, but with the full knowledge of the King. I returned her to her family and informed Hasan of what had occurred, and that I had avenged her disgrace. I never sought her love. I did not know she would follow me. Even had I returned her feelings, such a match would have been impossible. She was a noble Saracen and I merely a poor knight. Her interest flattered me, but I did not encourage it. Hasan knows this. I did the only honourable thing in going to him and giving him the opportunity to punish me if he so wished, but he knew that none of it was at my seeking. His sister was a foolish, passionate child, led astray by her romantic heart. And in the end she, too, took the honourable path, which her people understand. Death was her only choice.'

A great weight of shame and unshed tears choked Judith's throat, so that she was unable to speak. She sat looking at him dumbly, wishing unsaid all the cruel words she had flung at him.

'I am weary to my soul,' he sighed. 'I must sleep.' Heaving himself further onto the divan, he lay sprawled across the fur covers, while Judith let the slow tears fall silently from her eyes, trailing paths of misery down her face.

Mariamne dead. It was not an end Judith would have wished for her. Inside herself she found only pity for a hot-blooded girl who had thrown away everything in the name of love and come to such a sad fate. Judith hardly dared think of the torments Mariamne must have been through before that final, fatal night.

'I never sought her love,' Geoffrey had said. 'I did not encourage it.' And his voice had held the firmness of truth. If only she could have believed it before! Not that it would have altered anything. If he had not loved Mariamne neither did he love the woman whom he had been forced to marry, nor was there any future for such a marriage. Judith had no dowry and Geoffrey no fortune. He would remain in Outremer and she would return to

England. Married or unmarried, it made no difference.

So why had he brought her here? The question remained unanswered.

Alerted by an increase of light as the tent-flap was drawn back, Judith looked round to see a male slave bringing a tray of fruit and a pitcher of goat's milk. She signalled the man to be silent and he nodded gravely, bowing before stepping forward to set the tray on the low table; then he moved to where a chest stood, opening it to show her the contents—clothes in bright hues, of silk and muslin. He poured water into a bowl on a stand and laid beside it a towel as if inviting her to refresh herself. Bowing again, he departed as silently as he had come.

Moving with equal noiselessness, Judith stood up and went to splash water onto her tear-stained face before examining the neatly-folded garments in the chests—the gifts from Hasan's wives. She found beaded jackets, silken trousers, thin cotton gowns decked with embroidery and gems, silk robes and muslin surcoats, all in jewelled colours. Fingering the clothes admiringly, she wondered at Hasan's motives for providing her with such apparel. Did he assume that she would wish to appear desirable for her husband, as a Saracen woman would?

She glanced to where Geoffrey lay soundly asleep, veiled by muslin curtains. As she moved closer to the bed she was caught by a wave of unbearable tenderness towards him. How vulnerable he looked, his limbs spread across the furs, his face drawn with the effects of illness and sorrow. Recalling that time in Megiddo, she wondered if he might still respond to her womanhood, as a man must in his need. She was, after all, his wife.

With constant glances to make sure he was undisturbed, she moved a screen so that it would hide her from the tent entrance, removed her dusty clothes and washed herself all over in the scented water. A vial of perfume stood by the ewer—Hasan had missed no detail of hospitality—and she used it liberally before selecting a silken robe of golden hue lavishly embroidered with gold thread. It clung to her slender curves as she fastened it with a silk girdle around her waist; then she sat down to unbraid her hair, combing it until it flowed round her shoulders in thick, silvery waves.

As twilight deepened, the slave reappeared to light the lamps and bring more food—plates of rice with a vegetable mixture, meat on skewers, sweetmeats decorated with nuts and spices. The exotic, appetising aroma of the food, mingled with the tang of incense, must have disturbed Geoffrey for he sat up suddenly, looking round in the golden light that lay in pools around the tent.

'Supper is prepared,' Judith said softly, hot blood flooding her head. Suddenly she felt shy of him, nervous of his reaction to the way she was dressed. If he scorned her now she would never forgive him.

'I can smell it,' he said, rolling from the divan to stretch himself. He took a step towards her and stopped, his glance sweeping her as she sat on the cushions by the table, the silk robe softly caressing her breasts and the outline of her thighs. He said softly, questioningly, 'My lady?'

'Best wash your hands,' she instructed, avoiding his eyes. 'Are you rested?'

'Aye. And hungry, it seems. Excuse me.'

She heard him splashing water behind the screen and when he emerged he had thrown off the striped robe. His shirt was untied at the throat and a crimson sash spanned his waist, bright against the white linen of shirt and Turkish trousers. Giving her one swift, unreadable look, he came to settle himself cross-legged on the opposite side of the table and they began to eat.

He appeared to have been starving, but Judith's appetite had fled. Her stomach felt tied in nervous knots and she was vividly aware of her husband, his skin brown against the white garments he wore, his long fingers dipping into dishes with eager relish.

'You are not eating,' he observed. 'Is the food not to your taste?'

'It suits me well enough,' she replied. 'I am not very hungry. Sir, I—I have done you a grave injustice. I listened to ill-informed gossip. I beg you to forgive me for my hasty words.'

'Which particular hasty words?' he asked drily.

Her head came up. She opened her mouth to make some sharp retort, but the sight of his sparkling eyes gave her pause and she found herself unable to face him directly. 'All of them,' she muttered.

'That is a great deal to forgive all at once,' he said.

Pique gave her courage to lift her eyes again. 'I do not need reminding of the many times I have let my tongue have its way! Can you not accept an apology that is sincerely meant?'

'You must give me time to consider it. My lady, this humility is a new thing in you. Has the incense affected you?'

She had a feeling he might be teasing her, but his bland expression gave no hint of it. All she knew was that her temper was in danger of loosing its bonds. A pulse throbbed in her temple and her palms felt damp with nervousness, but she gritted her teeth and determined to say all the things she had intended to say.

'I wish also to thank you for saving my brother's life. He told me how you came to his rescue, at grave risk to yourself.'

'The action was forced upon me,' he replied with a shrug.

'You mean—you did it without thinking?'

'No, indeed I do not. I was thinking very clearly. Edwin is the heir to Claverham. He had to be saved, if only to demonstrate that I have no desire to claim your father's lands.'

Her face burned with humiliation. 'I never believed that to be true, my lord.'

'No? But you flung the accusation at me several times.'

'I remember!' she flared. 'I have asked you to forgive me. And you have not always played the gentle knight with me.'

'No. I remain my father's son. A de Belgarde.'

'The Earl's son you may be,' she said quietly, 'but you are not made in his image. You are your own man. I know that now, my lord.'

For a moment he was silent, regarding her with grave eyes in whose depths twinkled a demon of mischief— unless it was a trick of the lamplight. 'Twice now you have addressed me as your lord. Did you realise it?'

'It is the way a woman should address her husband,'

she muttered, her colour deepening, her eyes dark as night.

'Aye, when she is obedient to him. You have never been obedient to me, Judith. Always you fight me, and flay me with your tongue. And not many hours ago you were anxious to leave me and sail home to England.'

Restlessness drove her to her feet, to seek the cool night air at the tent entrance. The soft breeze breathed gently on her heated face and overhead the moon shone down, almost at the full, like a worn silver coin.

She flinched as Geoffrey's tall form loomed behind her and he reached across her to close the flap, saying, 'Our friends will be shocked if they see you thus attired, my lady. That robe is near transparent with the light behind it—a sight only a husband should see.'

She moved away, unnerved by his nearness, aware of his warmth and the male odour of his body, but wherever she stood there seemed to be a lamp nearby and Geoffrey's roving gaze proved the truth of his statement. She felt even more unsettled, for she had forgotten the effect he could have on her senses when he was in this lazy, seductive mood.

Smiling to himself, he fastened the laces that would enclose them in privacy, preventing anyone from entering the tent. 'One thing you might like to know. I have had letters from home, from my brother Waldin, Earl of Brecon.'

'Earl of—' She stared incredulously at him. 'Your father is dead?'

'He died in the springtime. I cannot grieve for him. He was as harsh a father as he was an overlord and I had not seen him for seven years. But you see, my lady, fate has put an end to his plotting. Waldin is not so ambitious. Besides, he has married a wealthy heiress who will bring him lands enough to add to his estates. He will not concern himself over the manor of Claverham. So Edwin may return, if he wishes.'

Judith could hardly believe the news. She had spent the whole summer dreading that Earl Torquil's evil might reach out to harm her brother, or herself, and the Earl had no longer been alive to harm anyone.

'Edwin said he would not go back to Castle Belgarde,' she said dazedly.

'But he must be given the choice. Or perhaps he would prefer to let *me* train him in the ways of chivalry. It could be arranged with Lord Guy.'

'You, sir?' She could not follow his reasoning.

'Oh, come, Judith,' he said with a wry smile. 'Not "sir". Say "my lord", and mean it.'

Although he made no move towards her, she felt a sudden urge to escape for his presence filled the tent with a delicious menace that made her senses reel. She looked around for somewhere to hide—something to protect her.

'Are you afraid of me?' he asked.

'No!'

'You look to be on the point of flight, like a captured bird battering its wings in a cage . . . Judith!'

His voice whipped across her taut nerves, startling her into stillness. She faced him squarely, her hands clenched at her sides, her whole being trembling as he walked slowly towards her with that feline grace which stirred her into heightened awareness of his strength and masculinity.

Pausing a little distance away, he brushed his hand against her cheek, making her flinch and quiver. His brow furrowed in response, his eyes narrowing.

'If you do not fear me, why do you shake so? I have been ungentle with you in the past, but it need not be so. I am only harsh when you anger me. Come, why did you perfume yourself and comb out your hair—' he stroked the shining waves, letting his hand brush her breast as if by accident, and Judith shuddered helplessly '—if not to please me?' he concluded.

'When—when you were asleep,' she faltered, 'you looked so weak and ill. I thought to—to offer you comfort, if you wished it.'

'And now?'

'Now, I—I am not sure. If you . . . if we . . . It might be more difficult to acquire an annulment if—'

'If we are truly wed by the uniting of flesh?' he asked softly, making her blush to the tips of her ears. 'Indeed it would make things awkward, if not impossible. I could not swear you were a virgin if I knew you were not. You would have to remain my wife.'

'Yes,' she whispered.

'Because of a weak moment when you pitied me,' he added, a hint of acerbity creeping into his tone.

That sour note brought Judith partially out of the spell that had gripped her, making her temper rise again. 'That is not what I said! It was not pity!'

'Then what name would you give it?' He laid a hand on her shoulder and with the other tilted her chin upward, obliging her to meet his compelling gaze.

Her mouth trembled but she could not form the word that drummed in her mind. Her eyes grew wide, filled with anguish that told, more clearly than speech, of her emotions, and she saw his face change as he read the silent message.

A groan that might have been her name escaped him as he bent his lips to hers and she flung her arms round his neck, meeting his hunger with demands of her own, her body melting against his even before his arms pressed her closer. Too long she had waited for him, worried about him, wanted him. Now nothing could prevent her from revealing her secret heart, not pride, not shame. Nothing.

After a long moment he lifted his head and said shakily, 'Dear love, can it be true? Tell me I am not dreaming, as I dreamed so often in fevered sleep. Are you here in my arms? Do you love me?'

'I do, my lord and my life.' Weeping, she buried her face in the warm curve of his throat, her lips against a pulse that pounded there. 'Make me your wife, even if it is to be for only a day. Give me memories to take with me behind the cloister door.'

'I may give you more than memories,' he murmured in her ear.

'I care not!' In an agony of tenderness, she kissed the vein that jumped beneath his brown skin, her body on fire as she leaned against him and knew he shared her desire. 'Geoffrey! Geoffrey!'

He bent suddenly and swept her off her feet, carrying her to the bed where at last he made full, sweet love to her, thrilling her to her soul.

But afterwards as she lay in his arms she could not stop weeping. She covered him with kisses, letting her tears bathe the livid scar where the lance had pierced him.

'Nay, love, do not weep so,' he murmured, a gentle hand stroking her nakedness.

'I must,' Judith sobbed. 'How can I bear to leave you now? Must I go? Oh, let me stay, my dearest lord! Let me go to Jaffa and wait on Baron Guy's wife. If I knew you were not far away . . . If we could be together sometimes : . .'

He threw her onto her back, leaning over her with his hands either side of her face and his body warm against her. In the soft lamplight his eyes gleamed with a tender amusement she had never seen there before.

'I see I forgot to tell you,' he said. 'I too am going to England. The King has rewarded me generously for my services, and Salah-ed-Din was equally pleased with my help in arranging peace terms. We shall have lands of our own, love—lands for our sons and rich dowries for our daughters. I am become a wealthy man. You shall be mistress of a castle, not an unwilling inmate of a nunnery.'

She stared up into his laughing eyes, her heart thudding as she began to believe that dreams might come true. 'You wish me—really wish me—to be your wife?'

'Can you doubt it? It would have been easy enough to be rid of you. But I did not want to lose you, Judith.'

'But you have been so angry with me!'

'With just cause, you must agree,' he said, only half-teasing. 'Oh, you were like an itch that refused to be cured by scratching. I did not know what ailed me—until I thought you drowned that night. Then I understood myself, and yet it seemed hopeless. I had nothing to give you, no means of supporting a wife. All I could do was set myself to deny my heart and free you from a marriage you appeared to detest. But it has been difficult, love.'

Feeling his body stir against her, she laughed softly. 'I know. Did you truly plan to be a monk? Celibacy would have been a real penance for you, Mountain Lion.'

'And you were not made to be a nun,' he murmured.

As he bent over her, Judith gasped with discomfort and clawed at the small round object that pressed into her back. It was the opal, still on its chain though one of the slender links had broken unnoticed at some point in their passionate embraces. Sighing, she let the gem dangle in the air.

'What shall I do with this?'

'Keep it. Give it to our eldest daughter. And tell her how a Saracen prince desired you for your wondrous beauty, Lady of the Moon. Say that I was near mad with jealousy.'

'Were you?' she asked, twining her hands into his hair.

'I was,' he assured her, and bent to kiss her softly, adding with wondering humour, 'Faith! You can work miracles it seems. A few hours ago I was a sick man, but you do me more good than any doctor's potion. Before we leave this place I shall be fit again.'

'Then let me give you more medicine,' she whispered, drawing his mouth down to hers.